W9-BUX-137

"Do not make this any more difficult. You need to get out of here."

Dante's brows, dark, straight and thick, lifted above mocking polished-ebony eyes. "Why?"

"How can you ask that?"

He casually levered himself into a sitting position with a distracting display of contracting muscles in his washboard stomach. "I really don't see what your problem is."

Eyes indignantly wide, Beatrice managed to drag them upward. Not that the breadth of his muscled shoulders and chest offered much respite for her wildly surging hormones.

"What?" he prompted, with an innocent look and a seemingly mystified shrug that intensified her murderous glare. "Unless you have forgotten, we are married."

Kim Lawrence lives on a farm in Anglesey with her university-lecturer husband, assorted pets who arrived as strays and never left, and sometimes one or both of her boomerang sons. When she's not writing, she loves to be outdoors gardening or walking on one of the beaches for which the island is famous—along with being the place where Prince William and Catherine made their first home!

Books by Kim Lawrence

Harlequin Presents

A Ring to Secure His Crown
The Greek's Ultimate Conquest
A Cinderella for the Desert King
A Wedding at the Italian's Demand
A Passionate Night with the Greek

Spanish Secret Heirs

The Spaniard's Surprise Love-Child
Claiming His Unknown Son

Visit the Author Profile page
at Harlequin.com for more titles.

Kim Lawrence

WAKING UP IN
HIS ROYAL BED

PAPL
DISCARDED

HARLEQUIN
PRESENTS

If you purchased this book without a cover you should be aware that this book is stolen property. It was reported as "unsold and destroyed" to the publisher, and neither the author nor the publisher has received any payment for this "stripped book."

HARLEQUIN®
PRESENTS®

PLEASE RECYCLE · THIS PRODUCT IS RECYCLABLE

Recycling programs for this product may not exist in your area.

ISBN-13: 978-1-335-40336-0

Waking Up in His Royal Bed

Copyright © 2021 by Kim Lawrence

All rights reserved. No part of this book may be used or reproduced in any manner whatsoever without written permission except in the case of brief quotations embodied in critical articles and reviews.

This is a work of fiction. Names, characters, places and incidents are either the product of the author's imagination or are used fictitiously. Any resemblance to actual persons, living or dead, businesses, companies, events or locales is entirely coincidental.

This edition published by arrangement with Harlequin Books S.A.

For questions and comments about the quality of this book, please contact us at CustomerService@Harlequin.com.

Harlequin Enterprises ULC
22 Adelaide St. West, 40th Floor
Toronto, Ontario M5H 4E3, Canada
www.Harlequin.com

Printed in U.S.A.

WAKING UP IN
HIS ROYAL BED

To Jane and the "Artists Unlocked"

CHAPTER ONE

BEATRICE RESISTED THE instinct to fight her way through the layers of sleep, instead easing her body closer to the warmth of the hard male contours she was lying... *Male*... The shocked acknowledgement hit at the same moment a distant clatter was joined by the melodic voice of her sister, who had clearly recovered from her migraine of the previous night and was singing something catchy and irritating downstairs.

One of the major differences between them, beyond the fact her sibling was not blonde, did not have blue eyes and was frequently referred to as petite and delicate, was that Maya was a morning person who woke with a smile on her face and a spring in her step. She could also hold a tune, and finally Maya would never have woken up beside a man who had walked into a bar alone and walked out minutes later *not* alone!

A protective hand went to Beatrice's face before she conquered her sense of dread and opened her eyes, widening her fingers fan-like to peer through them.

Maybe it was all a bad dream—with some very good parts.

It wasn't a dream!

Connecting with the pair of dark polished ebony eyes framed by lashes too thick and curling for any man, containing a sardonic gleam that stared right back at her, she loosed a low moan, scrunched her own eyes tight and twisted away.

The reaction of the owner of the eyes and the body, which even fully clothed had had every woman in the bar regarding her with envy as she had left with him, prevented her rolling into a foetal bundle of denial.

In her head she had stiffened in reaction to the heavy arm thrown casually across her ribcage; in reality her body softened and the determination to put some distance between them was overwhelmed by a fresh surge of toe-tingling heat, as a voice as deep and sin-fully seductive as the warm breath against her earlobe sent sharp tingles outwards from the core of liquid warmth low in her belly.

'What's the hurry?'

Eyes closed, she loosed a quivering sigh

and then moaned as he brought his hard body suggestively up against the curve of hers, providing enough reasons not to go anywhere as her resistance to the heavy throb of desire that robbed her limbs of strength dissolved utterly.

For several long languid moments she allowed herself to enjoy the feel of strong, sensitive hands and clever fingers moving up her ribcage, tracing a line down her belly, causing her to suck in a shocked, excited breath, before lifting to cup the weight of one breast, his thumb rubbing across the tight, aroused peak.

'Stop it?'

Now where did that question mark come from? she wondered, feeling a stab of frustration when he did just that, pulling his hand away. An action that caused her to squirm backwards a little and catch the thumb of the hand that came to rest on the curve of her jaw between her teeth.

'Play nice, Bea.'

Before she could react to the husky remonstrance, she found herself flat on her back. It wasn't his superior strength that kept her breathless there—she could have easily slid from underneath him. There was air between their bodies as, hands braced flat on the pillow either side of her face, knees either side of her hips, his body curved above her.

She was pinned there as much by the hungry ache inside her as his predatory bold dark stare fastened onto her face, lingering on her lips that still felt swollen from the kisses that had continued last night, even as they had torn each other's clothes off as they had stumbled across the room to the bed.

Her eyes darkened at the memories of the passionate coupling. The stress of discovering him beside her was pushed to the fringes of her mind as she stared back. His face was really a total miracle. Perfect was too mild a word to describe the sculpted arrangement of his perfect bone structure, the deep golden tone of his skin, dusted on his hollow cheeks and square lower jaw by a shadow of dark sexy stubble, the sensuality of his mouth, the firm upper lip counteracted by the full sensual lower.

She blinked and cleared her throat. 'I don't want to play.' She husked the words out past the ache in her throat. It was true there was nothing light or playful about the ache. It was on a par with the need, the *craving* for oxygen as she opened her eyes and managed to disconnect from his stare, but only escaped as far as his mouth, which did an equal amount of damage to her nervous system.

The sharply etched angle of his carved

cheekbones, the hawkish dominance of his nose blurred as his head lowered. The first kiss was a warm, tormenting whisper across her parted lips, drawing a fractured moan from her throat. The second, still soft on the side of her mouth, drew her body up into an arch as she tried to deepen the pressure. The ones that followed increased the torment until, unable to bear it any longer, she reached up, her fingers sinking deep into the thick dark hair, her hands locking on the back of his head as she dragged his face downwards, glimpsing the glitter in his dark eyes, before she pressed her mouth to his and closed her eyes.

Restraint gone, they kissed with a wild hunger, and they fell back. Warm bodies sinuously twisting to deepen the contact, driven by a passion that drove every other thought from Beatrice's head.

'Bea, are you coming down or shall I bring your coffee up?'

Beatrice stiffened as she was jarringly jolted back to reality. Eyes scrunched, a moan of self-recrimination locked in her throat, as without a word she rolled away from the warm body she was pressed against.

'Weak…stupid…weak…stupid!' she mumbled, beating herself up verbally as she swung her long legs over the side of the bed and, with a sinuous, graceful swoop, grabbed a sheet that had at some point fallen on the floor. She didn't stop until she reached the far corner of the room, where she stood, shoulder blades pressed to the wall, holding the sheet against her body. It was an inadequate shield but better than nothing.

She glanced nervously at the door; a nightmare scenario played in her head of the door opening and Maya appearing.

'I'll be down just now!' she yelled. 'You need to go!' she whispered, transferring her agonised glance to the man lying in her bed.

He looked in no hurry to go anywhere any time soon as he rolled onto his back, tucking one hand behind his head, causing the light sheet that lay across his narrow hips to slide another inch lower. He was totally at ease with his naked state but she was not. He was a living, breathing sculpture of perfectly formed muscles and warm olive-toned skin—just looking at him made things shift deep inside her.

The mockery in his expression was not quite in tune with the dark frustration in his heavy-lidded eyes as his glance came to rest on the swell of her full breasts above the sheet she held clutched against herself.

As he watched her struggles to control the white swathe, he visualised the slim curves beneath the tented fabric. The smooth, warm scented skin, the silk touch of her long legs as they wrapped around him. The thousand razor cuts of desire that came with the memory darkened his eyes to midnight.

'That is not what I need, *cara*.'

Before she was fatally distracted by the bold challenge of the seductive gleam in his heavy-lidded eyes, the timely interruption of her sister's voice drifting up the stairs again saved her from getting sucked back into the dangerous sexual vortex.

She clenched her even white teeth so hard she could hear the grind of enamel. She didn't feel saved at all, or maybe she didn't want to be saved?

'Oh, my God!'

He grinned a slow devilish smile of invitation.

'Oh, my God!' she whispered again with even more feeling as she realised how close she had come to accepting the invitation in his sinful eyes. She took a deep breath and thought, *Do not go there*. Her eyes flickered towards the figure in the bed—*again*!

Once was enough—actually it was too much! She cleared her throat. 'I'll be right down!'

she belted out, then directed an accusing glare at the figure occupying the bed, even though she knew the guilt was as much hers. When it came to Dante, why was she such a weak idiot? 'Do not make this any more difficult. You need to get out of here.'

His brows, dark, straight and thick, lifted above polished ebony mocking eyes. 'Why?'

'You can ask that?'

He casually levered himself into a sitting position with a distracting display of contracting muscle in his washboard belly. 'I really don't see what your problem is.'

Eyes indignantly wide, she managed to drag her gaze upwards, not that the breadth of his muscled shoulders and chest offered much respite for her wildly surging hormones.

'What?' he responded with an innocent look and a seemingly mystified shrug that intensified her murderous glare. 'Unless you have forgotten, we *are* married.'

CHAPTER TWO

HUFFING OUT A defiant gust of breath through clenched teeth, Beatrice refused to drop her gaze from the challenge she saw in the dark eyes of Dante Aristide Severin Velazquez, Crown Prince of San Macizo.

Her husband.

'If only I *could* forget.' Her mumble came with a resentful glare, at odds with the mood of their civilised divorce.

She never had really understood what a civilised divorce entailed, but she was pretty sure it did not entail having a night of passionate sex with your soon-to-be ex. But on the plus side, her peevish attitude did provide some sort of cover for her deep inner despair.

Everyone made bad choices, and she was no exception, but it sometimes felt that from the moment Dante had walked into her life the only sort of choices she'd made were of the bad variety—actually, *disastrous*!

She had always operated on the principle that your actions had consequences, and you lived with them. Or, in her case, you neatly plotted a course around them, or at least the more dangerous ones.

Then Dante happened and she forgot her philosophy; her navigation skills took a vacation. She didn't so much forget as didn't give a damn about the consequences. The primitive instincts that he had awoken in her were totally in charge. Instincts that had drowned out the warning bells that she had remained determinedly tone deaf to. Actually, last night there had been no bells, just a fierce *need*.

She had lifted her head and seen the reason why the crowded bar had fallen silent, and had felt a bone-deep desperation, much like any addict who found their drug of choice was close enough to smell. Dante was her addiction, the virus in her blood she had no antibody to.

Which made it seem as though she'd had no choice, but she had. She hadn't sleepwalked into the situation. She had known what she was doing every step of the way. Admittedly she had not typed his name into a search engine when she'd accepted the offer of dinner, knowing that he wasn't actually talking about a dinner. But you didn't need a bio to see at one glance that he represented the sort of danger she had spent her adult life avoiding.

The idea of experiencing an attraction strong enough to make her share intimacy with a man she didn't know had been a concept she had considered with a disbelieving smile, tinged, if she was honest, with smugness. But she'd had total confidence in her belief that any relationship she had would come from friendship and respect.

She'd slept with Dante that first night. She had been so determined to have that first night end the way she had imagined from the moment she had set eyes on him that she hadn't told him that this…that *he*…was her first, in case it made him back away.

Her instincts there had been bang on because Dante had not been pleased by the discovery she was inexperienced, sternly telling her that virgins were *not his thing* and demanding an explanation.

It could have ended there—it should have— but it hadn't, because she hadn't wanted it to.

When she had retorted that she wasn't a virgin any more so that was one obstacle gone she'd made him laugh, and he'd laughed again when she had explained that it hadn't been a conscious choice. She hadn't been waiting for the right man or anything, she simply wasn't a particularly *physical* person.

They had spent the next three days and nights in bed disproving this theory. Nothing and no one had disturbed them in the penthouse with million-dollar views that she'd never even looked at, and Beatrice had savoured every hot, skin-peelingly perfect moment of the intimacy because she'd known this heaven wasn't going to last. Dante had made that painfully clear.

He had left no room for misinterpretation when he'd explained that he was not into long-term relationships, or actually any sort of relationship at this point in his life.

Facts she'd already known, having finally typed his name into her phone's search engine—even if a tenth of the women he was alleged to have slept with were actually real, it would be amazing that he found time to be so hands-on with the charitable foundation that he had founded.

It made a person wonder if he ever actually slept, except she knew he did. She had watched him and been utterly fascinated by the way the strong lines on his face relaxed in sleep, made him look younger and *almost* vulnerable in a way that made her conscious of an empty ache inside her.

There had been more than one occasion over that weekend when he had felt the need to drag her feet back to earth by reminding her.

'This is just sex—you know that, right?'

The fantasy bubble she had spent the weekend in had ended when she'd opened her eyes and found him standing there, suited, booted and looking every inch the exclusive playboy prince who was always good for a headline.

She remembered fighting the self-respect-killing urge to run after him when he had stopped of his own volition, his long brown finger curled around the doorknob. She had managed a response as cool and offhand as his suggestion that they meet up in three weeks when commitments would be bringing him back to London.

By the time three weeks had come around things had changed, and the consequences of her actions had been impossible to ignore. Even without the multiple tests she'd *known* why she felt different; she'd known even without the blue line that she was pregnant.

She'd also known exactly how this next step was going to go, with a few gaps she'd left for his shocked, angry reaction. She had played the scene out in her head and, allow-

ing for a few variations, she'd known exactly
what she was going to say.

When she'd been buzzed into the building
she'd *still* known *what she* was going to say,
as she'd been escorted in the glass-fronted lift
by a silent suited man.

She'd walked in, and she'd known not just
what she was going to say but when she was
going to say it. She'd allow herself their *last*
night and then she would tell him.

In the event, the door had barely closed before she had blurted it out.

'I'm pregnant and, yes, I know we...*you*
were careful.'

She had a vague recollection of dodg-
ing his eyes, allowing her hair to act as a
screen to hide her guilty blushes. The memory even now had the power to make her insides squirm.

'I've done three tests and...no, that's a lie,
I did six. I am not...do *not* suggest *that*...
Just know that I want nothing from you. I'm
going home tomorrow to tell my mum and
sister and we'll be totally fine. I'm not alone.'

He had stood there totally motionless during her machine-gun delivery of the facts.
Strangely, saying it out loud had made the
secret she had nursed to herself seem slightly
less surreal.

She'd thought she'd been prepared for his every reaction, most had involved noise, but him turning on his heel and walking out of the door before she could even draw breath was not one she had been prepared for.

It might have been minutes or an hour, she didn't have a clue, but when the door had opened again she hadn't moved from the spot where she'd been before his abrupt departure. He had re-entered, still pale but not with shock now; determination as steely as his stare had been etched into the lines of his face.

'Well, obviously we need to get married. I don't need to involve my family in this—it's one of the advantages of being the spare. Carl is getting married and they probably won't even notice. How about you?'

Carl? What did his older brother have to do with this? *'Family...?'* Her thought processes had been lagging a confusing few steps behind his words.

'A big wedding, given the circumstances, is not an option, but if you want your immediate family to be there I can accommodate that. I have business in the area, so how does Vegas next week sound to you?'

He had paused, presumably for breath. She had definitely needed to breathe!

'You're not joking…? Dante, people don't get married because of a baby… Let's forget you ever said that. You're in shock.'

He didn't appear to appreciate her consideration. 'I may only be the spare but I am still second in line to the throne…*my* child will not carry the stigma of being a bastard. Believe you me, I've seen it and it's not pretty.'

'You're insane.'

Every argument she'd made against his plan he'd had a counterargument to. The most compelling one having been it was the right thing to do for the baby's sake, the new life that they had made.

She had ended up agreeing, of course. Saying yes to Dante was a habit she had to break if her life was going to get back on track.

As for last night! How could she have been that stupid *yet again*? And she had nobody to blame for it but herself! Dante didn't have to do anything to make her act like a lemming with her sights on a cliff edge, he just had to *exist*.

And nobody had ever *existed* as much as Dante—she had never met anyone who was *so* alive. He had a presence that was electrifying, and there was an earthy, raw quality to the megawatt vitality he exuded that made the idea of forgetting anything connected with him laughable.

But she had to. She had to put last night behind her and start again—it would get easier. It had to! First, she couldn't run and hide or pretend that last night didn't happen. She just had to accept she had messed up and move on.

Again...!

'What are you doing here, Dante?' Falling in love was not at all as she had imagined it—in fact it really should come with a health warning, or at least a misery warning!

'You invited me. It seemed rude—'

'How did you know where I was? How did you know we had gone away?' For the first few weeks after she had left Dante she had moved in with her mother, then she had taken residence on Maya's couch until a flat they could afford together had come up.

He arched a sardonic brow and she sighed.

'All right, stupid question.' She had considered fighting the insistence that she needed any sort of security, even the ultradiscreet team of men who in pairs watched her around the clock, but she had learnt that it was better to fight the battles you had a chance of winning. 'You know, there was a time when my life was my own.'

'It will be again.' Unlike Dante's. The moment his brother had stepped away from the line of succession had been the moment that Dante had known his life had changed forever. He was no longer the playboy prince and unexpected father-to-be. He was the future of the monarchy.

His flat delivery brought a furrow to her smooth wide brow, but his expression told her nothing. 'A friend of Mum's owns the place. We used to come here when we were kids.'

His glance lifted from his grim contemplation of his clenched hands and his future, as she glanced around the wood-lined walls of the modest ski lodge.

'Ruth, that's Mum's friend, had a last-minute cancellation and offered it to us for the fortnight for a song. Maya is working on ideas for a sports line and we thought the snow might inspire her.'

'So the business is going ahead? The fashion industry is notoriously tough.'

'Slowly,' she said, bringing her lashes down in a glossy protective sweep as he adjusted his position, causing a rippling of the taut muscles of his lean torso. He didn't carry an ounce of surplus flesh; his broad-shouldered frame would have made many a professional athlete sigh with envy.

She would have retreated if there had been any place to retreat to. Instead she ignored the pelvic quivering, and pretended her skin wasn't prickling, and tossed her hair as she adjusted her sheet once more.

'It would go a lot quicker and easier if you made the bank that is playing hardball aware of the settlement that will be yours. Do they even know you're going to be a very wealthy woman soon?'

Wealthy and single. She refused to acknowledge the sinking feeling in her stomach.

'And I'm more than happy to make the funds you need available to you now.'

Her lips tightened. If people called her a gold-digger that was fine, so long as she knew she wasn't. 'I don't want your money. I don't want anything—'

I want to go back to the person I was, she thought forlornly, aware that it was not going to happen. She might only have been married for ten months, and been separated for six more, but she could never be the person she was before, she knew that.

'Well, then, *cara*, you chose the right lawyer. Yours seemed more interested in golf than your interests.'

'Could you pretend, even for one minute, that

you don't know every detail of what's going on in my life? I repeat, why are you here?'

Good question, Dante thought as he dragged a hand through his hair, leaving it standing in sexy tufts across his head.

He'd told himself when Beatrice left that it would be easier if he could focus on his new role, without the distraction of worrying how she was coping, of knowing that behind her smile she was unhappy, resentful or usually both. That no matter how tough his day had been, hers had probably been worse.

Dante had never been responsible for another person in his life. He'd lived for himself, and now he had an entire country relying on him and Beatrice—that really was irony, of the blackest variety.

Except now she wasn't relying on him. The reports that landed on his desk all said as much. She was doing well…he had just wanted to see for himself. It was an option that would soon not be open to him. The list of potential successors to fill the space in his life Beatrice had left, candidates who would know how to deal with life inside the palace walls without his guidance, was already awaiting his attention. His stomach tightened in distaste at the thought of the breeding stock with good bloodlines.

'There are a few papers for you to sign,' he said, inviting her scorn with his lame response and receiving it as he skated around the truth in his head.

'And now you're a delivery service?'

He sighed out his frustration as his dark, intense gaze scanned her face hungrily. She was still the most beautiful thing he had ever seen in his life and for a while their lives had meshed. But things had changed. He had another life, responsibilities, duty. At some level had he thought coming here would offer him some sort of closure?

'We never actually said…goodbye.'

She blinked, refusing to surrender to the surge of resentment that made her heart beat louder. 'Didn't we? You probably had a meeting, or maybe you left me a memo?' She bit her lip hard enough to raise crimson pinpricks of blood. Could she sound any *less* like someone who had moved on?

'You felt neglected?'

'I felt…' She fought to reel in her feelings. 'It doesn't really matter. This was a conversation we never had, let's leave it at that. Let's call last night closure.'

He shook his head, the antagonism leaving his face as he registered the glisten of unshed tears in her eyes. His shoulders dropped. 'No, it wasn't planned. I just… I'm sick of receiving any news about you through third parties.'

'I miss…' She stopped, biting back the words she couldn't allow herself to admit to herself, let alone him. 'I think it's safer that way,' she said quietly.

'Who wants safe?'

The reckless gleam in his eyes reminded her of the man she had fallen in love with. There was an irony that she had to remind him he wasn't that man any more. 'Your future subjects and, frankly, Dante, I have all the excitement we can handle without…'

She closed her eyes and pushed back into the wall until the pressure hurt her shoulder blades. It was true—after she had walked away from the royal role she had never been equipped to fulfil, she had thrown herself into her life, and there were new, exciting and sometimes scary challenges to fill her days. She had recovered some of her natural enthusiasm, though these days it was mingled with caution. A caution that had been sadly missing last night. Dante walked into a room and all those instincts and hungers he woke in her roared into sense-killing life.

Senseless, she thought, underlining the second syllable in red in her head. Last night had had nothing to do with sense. Her insides tightened as the warm memories flooded her head. It'd had everything to do with passion, craving and hunger!

So she had a passion for chocolate, but if she gave into that indulgence Beatrice knew she'd need a new wardrobe. Exercise and a bit of self-control meant she could still fit into last year's clothes.

The trouble was Dante was a perfect fit, in every sense of the word, and he always had been.

When in one of her more philosophical moments she had told herself that she would take away the good bits from her marriage, she had not intended it this literally. Though even when everything else was not working in their marriage the sex had still been incredible. The bedroom was one place they always managed to be on the same page. Unfortunately, you needed more than sexual chemistry and compatibility for a marriage to work, especially when it had hit the sort of life-changing roadblocks theirs had.

With a self-conscious start she realised that during her mental meanderings her glance had begun to drift across the strong sculpted breadth of his chest, and lower, to the ridged muscular definition of his belly, before she realised what she was doing, and brought her lashes down in a protective sweep. Not that they provided much protection from the raw sexual pulse he exuded, or his unnerving ability to read her mind.

'Do you regret it?'

Her response to the question should have been immediate, a reflex, and of course she did regret what had happened, on one level. But on another, shameful level she would not have changed a thing, because Dante bypassed her common sense. She only had to breathe in the scent of his skin to send her instincts of self-preservation into hibernation.

I really *have to break this cycle!*

Easy to say, easy to think, but less *easy* when every time he touched her something inside her said it was *right*.

Then don't let him touch you!

Cutting off her increasingly desperate internal dialogue, Beatrice cleared her throat to give herself time to think of a next move that would manage to convey that last night didn't mean she wasn't totally over him. An action that wouldn't draw attention to the skin-prickling awareness and the warm pelvic heaviness.

A next move that established that she could walk away just as easily as he could after satisfying a primal itch. That he wasn't the only one who could compartmentalise his life.

'Last night was—'

His deep voice, the edges iced with impatience, cut across her before she could establish anything. 'Considering you are standing there huddled in a sheet, acting like some outraged virgin, I'm taking that you regret last night as a given.'

The accusing note in his voice brought a tinge of angry colour to her cheeks.

'That's really astute of you,' she drawled sarcastically. Where Dante was concerned her virginal outrage had always been zero, even when she'd had a right to the title. She had had no qualms about giving him her virginity, though he had been a lot less *relaxed* about receiving the unexpected gift.

'Do you regret marrying me?' Asking the second time did not make it any clearer to him why her answer mattered to him…except to lessen his guilt, maybe?

The irony was not lost on him. There could be few people who had spent a life where guilt featured less heavily… His upper lip curled in a bleak smile.

If he'd been a man who believed in karma he might think that his present situation was Fate's way of making him pay for an empty life of utter hedonism. Where the only way was the easy way. Having once rejected the concept of duty, now he was ruled by it.

He'd imagined that he was doing the *right thing* when he had proposed, never for one moment asking himself what the right thing was for Beatrice. He'd been the one making the ultimate sacrifice. Unwilling to own his thoughts, jaw clenched, he pushed out a breath through flared nostrils.

She blinked, her long lashes brushing the smooth curve of her cheeks like butterfly wings. 'There's no point regretting, is there?'

'Which means you do.' Did she ever ask herself if things might have ended differently if their baby had clung to life and not simply been a heartbeat that had vanished from the screen?

His guts tightened like an icy fist as the memory surfaced of the doctor relaying the news alongside the information that the baby had just faded away.

He had been consumed by a devastation that had felt as if he were being swallowed up. It had made no sense. He'd never wanted children—hadn't wanted a child.

'I'm looking forwards.'

His glance lifted as his thoughts shifted back to the present moment.

The intensity of his stare made Bea lose her thread, but after a momentary pause she managed to regain control and her defiance.

'The past is done and gone. I'm not interested in revisiting—' She felt the sheet slip and yanked it up. As she did the colour seeping under her skin deepened the golden-toned glow as the irony of what she was about to claim hit her. Sometimes honesty, wise or not, was the best, or only, policy.

Her shoulders lowered as the defensive antagonism drained away, exposing the vulnerability that lay beneath. Dante looked away but not before he felt something twist hard in his chest.

'I have a lot of lovely memories that I will always treasure. I'm just not as realistic as you are sometimes.' She bit down on her quivering lower lip before the emotion took her over.

A spasm played across the surface of his symmetrical features that had more than once been called *too* perfect. 'Maybe I have lower expectations… You should try it, Beatrice. Less disappointment in life,' he suggested harshly.

'You want me to be as cynical as you are? That's a *big* ask, Dante.'

Heavy eyelids at half mast, his eyes gleaming, he quirked his mobile lips into a mocking smile that invited her to share his joke as their eyes connected. 'You call it cynicism. I call it realism, and it's all about baby steps, *cara*.'

It wasn't just her expression that froze, time did too. He could almost hear the seconds count down before her lashes came down in a protective sweep, but not before he had seen the hurt shimmer in her eyes.

Jaw clenched, he silently cursed himself. Of course he knew the self-recrimination might have been of more use if it had come sooner. Like when the loss of their baby had become not a personal tragedy, but one debated by palace mandarins and *sources* close to the throne.

It had come as no surprise to him—he'd known the moment his brother stepped away from the throne what lay ahead for him. But to Beatrice it must have felt like an alternative universe.

She waited for the toddler in her head with Dante's eyes to take his first faltering steps before she let the image go and looked up, ignoring the ache inside her. Dante didn't meet her eyes—maybe he was thinking about the *practical princess* he would replace her with…the one that could give him babies.

The babies she had tried so hard to give

him; ten months of married life within the palace walls and ten months of waiting and hoping, then the awful inevitable sense of failure.

He swung his legs over the side of the bed, causing the rumpled sheet across his middle to slide a few treacherous inches lower.

Fighting the dormant protective instincts that Beatrice woke in him, Dante shrugged, but the truth was the thing she actually needed protecting from was him.

'I'm sorry.'

Cheeks hot, eyes wary, she dragged her wandering gaze up from his muscled thighs, but his expression was frustratingly hard to read.

'For what?' If he said he was sorry for last night she would hit him, she vowed grimly. 'Marrying me? I knew what I was doing,' she retorted, not happy at being cast in the role of victim.

'And now you're getting on with your life.' *Without him.*

'That might be easier if you weren't sitting in my bed.'

'I need to be in Paris tomorrow. The meeting was delayed and—'

'You wanted to mess my life up some

more?' There was more weariness than re-
proach in her voice.

'I didn't invite myself into your bed, Beatrice.'

Colour scored her cheeks. Did he really
think she needed that spelt out? 'Sorry. I'm
not blaming you. You've been very good
about making it easy for me to leave.

'So are there any papers?'

'There are papers, but…'

'But?'

'The tabloids love to—'

She tensed, suddenly seeing where this
was going, and why he wasn't quite meeting
her eyes. Pale but composed, she cut him off.
'Congratulations.'

His brows knitted into a perplexed frown.
'For what?'

'You're *engaged*…?' Her racing thoughts
quickly joined the dots, swiftly turning the
theory in her head to fact in seconds. It would
be something official. He wouldn't have come
all this way to tell her in person that he had a
lover. She had kind of taken that for granted.
A sensual man like Dante was not built for
celibacy.

His steady stare told her nothing, but she
knew and she was totally fine with it, or she
would be if she didn't throw up.

'Aren't you?'

Finally, a low hissing sound of amazement escaped his clenched teeth. 'Engaged would be a little premature. I'm not divorced yet.'

Her eyelashes flickered like butterflies against her cheeks. 'Oh, I just…'

'Made one of your leaps based on the well-known scientific theory that if something is totally crazy it is true.'

'It was a perfectly reasonable assumption,' she retorted huffily, hating that she felt almost sick with relief, but adding for her own benefit as much as his, 'You will get remarried one day—you'll have to.'

His gut twisted in recognition of the accuracy of her words *have to*. She said *have to*—the people around him, his family, the courtiers, called it duty. Every word he spoke, his every action would be observed and judged. *He* would be judged.

The bottom line was his life was no longer his own. Even as he opened his mouth to respond Dante recognised the hypocrisy of his occupation of the moral high ground. 'So, you think that I'd be engaged and sleep with you?'

'Yes,' she said without hesitation, the damning shame curdling inside her reserved for herself, not him, because she knew that nothing would have stopped her sleeping with

Dante last night. 'You'd only be keeping up the family tradition,' she sniped.

One corner of his mobile lips quirked upwards as he remembered how shocked she'd been when she'd realised that his parents both had lovers who upon occasion slept over. His normality was her shocking.

'Will you sit down? I'm not about to leap on you.'

'No.' She backed a little further into the corner. It wasn't *him* she was worried about; they were both naked, and sitting was just one touch away from lying down. Her eyes widened as another equally and actually more probable explanation for his presence occurred to her. 'Is this about the divorce?' Her voice rose a shrill octave as she gulped and tacked on, 'Is there a problem?'

'No, it is not about the divorce. It is about Grandfather.'

'Reynard?' She stopped nervously pleating the fabric she held tight across her breasts and smiled. The old King, who had stepped back from the throne in favour of his son, Dante's father, after he suffered a stroke. Reynard had been one of the very few people she had been able to relax around in the palace.

Known for his acerbic tongue and a wit that took no prisoners, he'd made Beatrice laugh, though she had not realised until after the fact that being taught chess by him was considered a rare privilege.

They still played chess online. 'One of these days I'm going to beat him.'

One corner of Dante's mouth lifted in a half-smile. 'If you ever do it'll be for real. He won't let you win.'

'I hope not... So how is he?' She read enough in his face to make her panic; it wasn't so much his expression that made her heart lurch, more the careful lack of it. 'Oh, my God, he's not...not...?'

'No...no...he's all right,' Dante soothed.

She had barely released a sigh of relief when he added, 'He has had another stroke.'

'Oh, God, no!'

'Don't panic, the doctors gave him the clot-busting stuff in time, so they say there's no permanent damage, no further damage at least.'

She huffed out a sigh of relief but still felt shaky and sad because one day her worst-case scenario would be true, and a world without that irascible character would be a lesser place.

'We've kept everything in-house but it's in-evitable that the news is bound to leak soon, and you know how they play up the drama disaster angle. I wanted you to know the facts, not the exaggerated fiction.'

'Why didn't you just say this was why you came?' His eyes captured her own and Beatrice felt the blush run over her skin. 'All right,' she cut in quickly before he could point out that last night had not involved much talking. 'You could have messaged me...rung...?'

'Yes, I could.' He released her eyes suddenly.

'It wasn't kind coming here. This hasn't been easy for me...'

His jaw clenched. 'You think it has for me?' he pushed out in a driven tone.

'Right, so let's just call last night goodbye.' It had to be because she couldn't do this more than once. 'Give my love to Reynard. I really wish I could see him. He *really* is all right?'

'He really is. You *could* see him.'

Beatrice gave a bitter laugh. 'Come back to San Macizo? I presume you're joking.'

'Were you so unhappy there?'

She kept her expression flat. 'I was irrelevant there.' The only function that would have made her acceptable was producing babies and she hadn't done that. The month after month of raised expectations and then... Dante must have been relieved when she had announced that she'd had enough. The recognition made her throat tighten; she ignored it.

She was ignoring so hard she nearly tripped over the draped sheet. Enough was enough!

Head high, not glancing in his direction, she stalked across to the wardrobe and, presenting him with her back, pulled the turquoise silk robe from its hanger on the door.

There was a sheer ridiculousness to her display of false modesty around Dante, who knew every inch of her body—intimately. She let the sheet fall.

'I tried for ten months,' she said, throwing the words lightly over her shoulder, glad that he couldn't see her face. 'I tried to do the *right* thing, say the right thing. I tried to fit in. I tried...' She didn't finish the sentence, but the unspoken words hung between them like a veil. They both knew what she had tried and failed to do, the only thing that would have made her acceptable to his family: provide an heir.

CHAPTER THREE

BACK TURNED TO HIM, Beatrice tightened the sash before she turned, doing her best to not notice the molten gleam in his eyes as he watched her cinch the belt a little tighter.

She tilted her chin to a defiant angle and tossed her hair back from her face before tucking it behind her ears as she stomped over the sheet, her pearly painted toenails looking bright against the pale painted boards scattered with rustic rugs.

Despite the snow that had begun to fall again outside, the temperature was if anything too warm, thanks no doubt to the massive cast-iron radiator that didn't seem to respond to the thermostat.

Pretty much the way her internal thermostat ignored instructions when Dante was in the vicinity.

'You were the one who was hung up on that.'

The claim made her want to throw something at him.

'You were never irrelevant. A pain in the... but never irrelevant,' he drawled, unable to stop his eyes drifting over the long sensual flow of her body outlined under the silk. 'Have I seen that before? It brings out the colour of your eyes.' Which were so blue he'd initially assumed that she wore contact lenses.

She sketched a tight smile. 'It's been six months. I've added a few things to my wardrobe. You probably have a list somewhere.'

'Six months since *you* left, Beatrice. I didn't ask you to go.'

She'd left. It was not an option for him; he could never walk. He was trapped, playing a part. He would be for the rest of his life. Typecast for perpetuity as a person he would never be.

Beatrice felt her anger spark, the old resentments stir. He made it sound so simple, and leaving had been the hardest thing she had ever done. How much simpler it would have been if she had stopped loving him, how much simpler it was for him because he never had loved her, not really.

It was a truth she had always known, a truth she had buried deep.

'You didn't try and stop me.'

'Did you want me to?'

'Even if I had got pregnant, a baby shouldn't be used to paper over the cracks in a relationship, which is why this can't happen again.'

'*This...?*'

'This, as in you turning up and...' She caught her eyes drifting to his mouth and despaired as she felt the flush of desire whoosh through her body. This *need* inside her frightened her; she didn't want to feel this way. 'I think in the future any communications should be through our solicitors,' she concluded, struggling to keep her voice clear of her inner desperation, making it as cold as she could.

Dante felt something tighten in his chest that he refused to recognise as loneliness, as he pushed back fragments of memories that flashed in quick succession through his head. The tears in his brother's eyes as he said sorry, the coldness in his parents' eyes as they informed him that the future of the royal family rested on his shoulders.

'So, you don't think that exes can be friends.'

Her hard little laugh sounded unlike the full, throatier, uninhibited laugh he remembered. A few weeks into their marriage and she hadn't laughed at all.

'This isn't friendship, Dante. Friends *share*.'

* * *

Share, she said. He almost laughed. The last thing he had wanted to do was share when he was with Beatrice. He had wanted to forget. He didn't want to prove himself to his wife; he was proving himself to everyone else.

For the first time in his life Dante had been experiencing fear of failure, something so alien to him that it had taken him some time to identify it. Worse than the weakness was the idea of Beatrice seeing those fears, looking at him differently… He knew the look. He had seen it every day and he couldn't have borne it.

He had seen that look in the eyes of the team who had been put in place to coordinate his own repackaging, even while they *told* him they had total confidence in him, before asking him to embrace values that he had long ago rejected. They appealed to his sense of duty.

The real shock, at least to him, was that he possessed one. He'd spent his life trying to forget the early lessons on duty and service, but it seemed that they had made a lasting impression.

He didn't share this insight, unwilling to give anyone the leverage this weakness would have afforded them. Instead he listened and then worked towards cutting the team down to three people he could work with.

He would have liked to get rid of the lot, but he was a realist. It had taken his brother a lifetime to recognise what he had grasped in weeks wearing the mantle of Crown Prince. You really couldn't have it all, you had to make sacrifices.

His glance narrowed in on Beatrice's lovely face. *What* you were prepared to sacrifice was the question.

'I can't be half in, half out, Dante, it's not… fair. It's cruel…' she quivered out.

His glance flickered across the lovely, anguished features of the woman he had married. Finally *seeing sense* was how his father had reacted when he had broken the news that they were splitting up.

'She has come to her senses. Beatrice is leaving me.'

Dante had pushed the fact home that this was her choice, though not adding that fighting the decision was about the only noble thing he had done in his life. Lucky for him *nobility* was not a prerequisite for the job of King-in-waiting, unlike hypocrisy.

He knew that he ought not to be feeling this rage, this sense of betrayal. Their marriage had been about a child, then there was no child. Beatrice's decision had been the logical one. He could not see why it had shocked him so much.

Most successful marriages owed their longevity to mutual convenience and laziness, or, as in his parents' case, they were business arrangements, two people living parallel lives that occasionally touched. This was not something that Beatrice could ever understand.

In the end, the official line had been trial separation, while behind-the-scenes lists of replacements were drawn up for when the *trial* was officially made permanent.

He wasn't much interested in the lists, or the names of those that were added, or deleted after a skeleton emerged from their blue-blooded closet.

One *suitable* bride was much the same as another to him, though he wondered if the woman who had been chosen to share the throne with his brother, and had unwittingly been his brother's tipping point, had been included. He could not remember her face or name, just that she belonged to one of the few minor European royal families he and Carl were not related to.

Carl had choked before it was made official, choosing to step away from the lie and his life...because though San Macizo was considered progressive, the idea of an openly gay ruler unable to provide an heir was not something that could be negotiated.

His option had been walk away, or live a lie.

Dante had wondered whether, if the situations had been reversed, he would have shown as much strength as his brother.

One of the things that had struck him, after his initial shock at the revelations, was that he *was* shocked that he really hadn't seen it coming. When his brother had revealed his sexual orientation and his deep unhappiness, Dante hadn't had a clue. But then he never had been much interested in anyone's life but his own, he acknowledged with a spasm of self-disgust.

There was an equal likelihood that he hadn't recognised his brother's struggles because it really wouldn't have suited him to see them.

His glance zeroed in on Beatrice's face, the soft angles, the purity of profile, the glow that was there despite the unhappiness in her eyes. Just as he had tried not to see Beatrice was unhappy.

'And you're out.' His shoulders lifted in a seemingly negligent shrug. 'Fair enough.'

She blinked, hard thrown by his response,

a small irrational part of her irked that he wasn't fighting. 'You agree?'

'I already did. We are getting divorced, so relax, things are in hand,' he drawled.

'Are they?' Yesterday she'd have agreed but yesterday she hadn't been breathing the same air as Dante. Since then she had been tested and had come face to face with her total vulnerability, her genetic weakness where he was concerned.

'It's in everyone's best interests for this to happen. We're all on the same page here.'

'Pity the same couldn't be said for our marriage.'

It shouldn't have hurt that he didn't deny it, but it did.

Her decision to leave had been greeted with thinly disguised universal relief, which gave a lie to the myth that divorce didn't happen in the Velazquez family. It made her wonder if there had been others before her who had been airbrushed from royal history.

'I don't think anyone expected it to last, not even you…?'

Dante shrugged and deflected smoothly. 'I never expected to get married. I think it has a very different meaning for us both.'

In his family marriage was discussed in the same breath as airport expansion, or hushing the scandal of a minister who had pushed family values being caught in a compromising position, and the latest opinion poll on the current popularity of the royal family—it was business.

His heart had always been shielded by cynicism, which he embraced, but maybe it was the same cynicism that had left him with no defence against the emotional gut punch that Beatrice and her pregnancy had been.

'You're right.' He unfolded his long lean length and stood there oblivious to his naked state before casually bending to retrieve items of clothing, throwing them on the bed before he began to dress.

She couldn't not look; his body was so perfect, his most mundane action coordinated grace. She just wished her appreciation could be purely aesthetic; just looking made her feel hungry and ashamed in equal measure.

'I am?' she said, the practical, sane portion of her mind recognising this was a good thing, the irrational, emotional section wanting him to argue.

He turned as he pulled up his trousers over his narrow hips, his eyes on her face as his long fingers slid his belt home.

'Our lives touched but now—' Touched but nearly not connected—maybe it had been the sheer *depth* of his reaction that had made him show restraint, and it had required every ounce of self-control he possessed not to seek the glorious woman with endless legs and golden skin he had seen across the crowded theatre foyer, or at least find out her name... but he had walked away.

When, days later, he had found himself in the front row of the catwalk show of the hottest designer of the season with...he really couldn't remember who he had arrived with, but he could remember every detail of the tall blonde under the spotlight drifting past, hands on her hips, oozing sex in a way that had sent a collective shiver of appreciation around the audience. She had been wearing an outfit that was intended to be androgynous but on her it really hadn't been—it had felt like Fate.

He had allowed his companion to drag him to the sort of back-slapping, self-congratulatory, booze-fuelled backstage party that he would normally have avoided, where he got to know her name, Beatrice, and the fact she had already left.

His companion, already disgruntled by the lack of attention, had stayed as he'd run out of the place...in the grip of an urgency that he hadn't paused to analyse.

An image of her face as he'd seen it that day supplanted itself across her features. She'd stood too far away then for him to see the sprinkling of freckles across her nose. But they'd been visible later, when he had literally almost knocked her down on the steps of the gallery where the fashion show had been held. She'd looked younger minus the sleeked hair and the crazy, exaggerated eye make-up and he had decided in that second that there was such a thing as Fate—he had stopped fighting it. Never before had he felt so utterly transfixed by a woman.

She didn't fit into any stereotype he had known. She was fresh and funny and even the fact she'd turned out to be virgin territory, which ought to have made him run for the hills, hadn't.

A clattering noise from downstairs cut into his reminisces and made Beatrice jump guiltily.

'How is Maya?' he asked.

'People are finally recognising her artistic talent.'

Her sister might think that talent spoke for itself but Beatrice knew that wasn't the case. That was where she came in. She had done night classes in marketing during her time modelling, while everything she'd earned during that period had gone into their start-up nest egg for their own eco-fashion range.

Dante grunted, in the act of fighting his way into his shirt. Beatrice willed her expression calm as his probing gaze moved across her face.

'Will you be all right?'

'I'll be fine.' She would be; she wasn't going to let her Dante addiction of a few months define her or the rest of her life. She had accepted that it would be painful for a while, but she was a resilient person by nature, strong. Everyone said so.

So it must be true.

When her dad had died people had said how strong she was, what a rock she was. Then when Mum had married Edward she had been there for Maya, who had been the target of their stepfather's abuse. For a time, she had been the only one who had seen what the man was doing, because there had been nothing physical involved as he had begun to systematically destroy her sister's self-esteem and confidence.

For a while their mother had chosen the man she had married over her daughters, believing his lies, letting him manipulate her, controlling every aspect of her life. It had been a bad time and for a long time Beatrice, more judgemental than her sister, had struggled to forgive her mother her weakness.

The irony was that marriage to Dante had shown her that the same weakness was in her, the same flaw. Dante hadn't lied, which perhaps made her self-deception worse. She had wanted to believe he was something he wasn't, that they had something that didn't exist.

She pushed away the memories, focusing on the fact that she and Maya had forgiven their mother; their bond had survived and so had they. Now all they both wanted was their happily divorced mum to stop feeling so guilty.

'And how are your parents?' She felt obliged to enquire but could not inject any warmth into the cool of her voice.

'Pretty much the same.'

She lifted her brows in an acknowledgement as the memory of that first-night dinner in the palace with his parents flashed into her head. The shoulder-blade-aching tension in the room had taken her appetite away, and, if it hadn't, the unspoken criticisms behind the comments directed her way by the King and Queen would have guaranteed she was going to bed hungry.

And alone.

It had been two in the morning before she'd sat up at the sound of Dante's tread. She remembered that waiting, checking the time every few minutes. In the strange room, strange bed, in a strange country it had felt longer.

She had switched on the bedside light.

'Sorry, I didn't mean to wake you.'

She remembered so clearly the empathy that had surged through her body when she saw the grey hue of exhaustion on his normally vibrantly toned skin. Her throat tightened now as she remembered just wanting to hold him. If that day had been tough for her, she had told herself, it must have been a hundred times worse for Dante.

'I wasn't asleep,' she'd said as he'd come to sit on the side of the bed.

'You were waiting up.'

She'd shaken her head at the accusation. 'You look so tired.' She'd run a hand over the stubble on his square jaw—he even made haggard look sexy as hell.

'Not too tired.' She remembered the cool of his fingers as he'd caught the hand she had raised to his cheek and pulled her into him, his whisky-tinged breath warm and on his mouth as he'd husked against her lips, 'I just want to…bury myself in you.'

She pushed away the memories that were too painful now. They reminded her of her own wilful stupidity—for her that night it had gone beyond physical release. Dante had always taken her to a sensual heaven, but this connection had gone deeper, she had told herself as she'd lain later, her damp, cooling body entwined in his, tears of emotion too intense to name leaking from the corners of her eyes. She had felt so…complete.

But it had been a lie, her lie, and the cracks had started to appear almost immediately—before their heated, damp bodies had finished cooling in the velvet darkness.

CHAPTER FOUR

BEA WAITED UNTIL he had finished dressing before voicing the question that had inserted itself in her head and wouldn't go away. If she didn't ask she knew from experience the anxiety would start to eat away at her.

'I was wondering…' She paused, wishing she possessed Dante's enviable ability to distance himself from negative emotions. The world could be falling apart, panic endemic, but Dante, all calm, reasoned logic, would stand apart.

'Wondering?'

'Will last night affect the divorce?' What was the legal take on sleeping with your *almost* ex-husband?

'That's what you're worried about?'

'Well, aren't you?'

He gave a twisted smile. 'Are you going to tell anyone about it?'

The colour flew to her cheeks. 'Of course not, though of course Maya will—'

'Will be waiting for our walk of shame.'

'Maya doesn't judge.' Or blab, which was just as well when you considered the things she had told her sister.

'Of course she doesn't.'

She ignored the sarcasm and pushed him for an answer. 'Well, will it?'

'I see no reason it should.'

'Right, so we can forget last night happened and get on with our lives.'

'You seem to be already doing that…'

Underneath the smooth delivery she picked up *something* in his voice, an unspoken *suggestion* that she shouldn't be. It brought a flare of anger and she embraced it, embraced anything that wasn't the emotions of this slow, never-ending, nerve-wracking goodbye.

'Well, I *thought* about sitting in a room and fading away, but then I thought there might be life after Dante and you know what—' she widened her eyes in bright blue mockery '—there is.'

Jaw clenched, Dante viciously shoved a section of shirt in the waistband of his trousers and dragged a hand across his hair. 'So, who is he?'

'Who…what…?' She expelled a little sigh

of comprehension as enlightenment dawned. This time she didn't need to jab her anger into life. 'Oh!'

For a split second she was tempted to invent an active love life—after all, she seriously doubted a man with Dante's appetites would have been celibate. His morals were certainly flexible enough for him to not allow something like a *nearly* ex-wife to keep him faithful.

Would he be jealous?

It was a sign that she had a long way to go in her journey to not caring to know that she wanted him to be.

'Does there always have to be a man?' she countered, viewing him with arch-browed disdain. 'I don't need a man to complete me! *Any* man! I am not my m—' She stopped before she voiced the comparison that was in her head.

It took a moment for his muscles to unclench and banish the image in his head of a faceless male exploring the delights of Beatrice's body. He'd get used to the idea, but it was too soon yet, which sounded like a rationalisation and was, which was new territory for a man who had never understood the concept of jealousy in relationships.

But now the idea of another man appreciating Beatrice's long lush curves, beautiful face, the shape and intensity of colour of her wide-spaced sapphire eyes, the wide, generous curve of her lips and the smooth pallor of her flawless creamy skin filled him with an impotent rage.

The idea of the laughter in her eyes and her deep, full-throttle, throaty laugh being aimed at someone who was not him made his grip on his self-control grow slippery.

'We should have had a wild passionate affair.' Wild passionate affairs had a beautiful simplicity. They burned bright, they hit a peak and they faded. Controlled madness that was temporary, that left no regrets, no sense of unfinished business.

His words made her flinch. 'Instead I got pregnant… The irony is, of course, that if we'd just waited there wouldn't have been a baby to get married for.'

His expression darkened. 'That wasn't what I meant, and you know it. I know you blame me for the miscarriage but—'

'I blame you?'

His lips twisted in a cynical half-smile that left his dark eyes bleak as he challenged, 'So you have *never* thought that if you hadn't been forced to transplant yourself to another country, an alien environment, being isolated from everything you knew, your entire support system, you might not have lost the baby?'

'I thought none of those things.' But it was clear from his expression that he did. Why had she never suspected that Dante felt guilt for the loss of the baby? 'The doctors told us that a high portion of pregnancies end early on—a lot of women don't even know there ever was a baby.'

'Stress plays a part in these things. And an affair would inevitably have burnt itself out and we could have parted friends.'

'I think we have already established that isn't going to happen. You do realise that that was spoken like a true commitment-phobe.'

Dante shrugged. He had no problems with the description, though it implied that he had been running or avoiding something, which he hadn't.

Dante had never felt anything that inclined him to believe that he was marriage material. He would, he had always suspected, make a terrible husband. Well, on that at least he had been proved right—he had been, and he was.

'You need to leave.' She caught her lower lip between her teeth, her eyes swivelling from him towards the door, recognising the danger, the anger between them often found release in a *physical* way.

'Yes, I do.'

It had all gone quiet downstairs but the main thing was making Dante vanish and failing that…there was no way she could smuggle Dante out without Maya seeing him. She paused mid thought, almost wanting to laugh that she had been considering the smuggling option!

About time you took responsibility for your own actions, she told herself sternly, knowing full well it wasn't Maya's judgement she was trying to dodge but her own. She tightened the belt on her robe, causing the neckline to gape and drawing his eyes like magnets to the smooth swell of her cleavage.

Beatrice swallowed. His eyelids had dropped to half mast; the gleam below made her throat dry.

'That's the exact same colour as the top you were wearing when we first met. You had something in your eye.'

'Did I? I don't remember,' she lied.

'You were making it worse, stabbing your eyes with that tissue. And swearing like a sailor. You bumped into me.'

'You bumped into me,' she contradicted, her breath coming fast as she remembered him taking the tissue from her fingers, ignoring her protests. *'Let me,'* he'd said and she had—soon she had let him do a lot more.

She'd *begged* him to do a lot more!

'You looked so—' Young, fresh and a million miles away from the sleek creature on the catwalk, but even more sexy without the dramatic make-up, her pale hair no longer sleeked back but loose. It had spilled like silk down her back. He should have realised then that she was an innocent but he hadn't, and when he had, it had been too late.

You think it would have made a difference? his inner voice mocked as he dragged himself back to the moment and watched as Beatrice shook her head.

The effort to escape the memories in her head hurt but it was worth it. She had moved on and, more importantly, *she would never become her mother.*

'So, we have an understanding. From now on any communication will be through our legal teams,' she said, making her voice cold.

'You don't have a team. You have a solicitor who spends more time watering his roses than looking after his clients' interests.'

Left to that guy Beatrice would be walking away from their marriage just as poor financially as she'd walked into it, if he had not issued some instructions that made his own legal team look slightly sick. There were some lawyers who recognised a moral scruple when they saw one, but none of them worked for the Velazquez family.

'Bea, shall I bring the coffee up?'

Dante watched as Beatrice responded to the voice that drifted up the stairs with an 'over my dead body' expression on her face, which she backed up with a dagger look.

Not analysing his motivation, he walked past her and pulled the door open.

'We'll be right down, Maya!' He let the door close with a snap.

Feet apart, hands on her hips, she fixed him with a glare of seething dislike. 'Well, thank you for that.'

'Call it a parting gift.'

'I'd call it a cheap shot.'

He sighed out his irritation. 'Would it be preferable for me to just appear? At least she's had some forewarning. Unless you were going to smuggle me out?'

Beatrice felt the guilty wash of colour stain her cheeks. 'Let's just get this over with. Don't say *anything*,' she hissed.

'Is there anything left to say?'

'I suppose not.'

Her expression was as blank as her voice. Once, he had been able to read everything she felt because she had worn her emotions so close to the surface. Was this what palace life had done to her?

What you did to her.

He'd set her free, which ought to make him feel good. It didn't, but then he'd always thought doing the right thing was overhyped.

Her sister, dressed in dark ski pants and a chunky cable sweater she wore with the sleeves rolled up, didn't turn as she continued to stir the scrambled eggs on the stove.

There was an unmistakable chill in the air.

'Good morning, Dante.'

'Dante was just—'

'Let's not go there, shall we?' Maya stopped stirring and turned, spoon in hand. She blanked Dante, which was something not many people could manage, and slanted a wry look across at her sister.

Beatrice bit her tongue, though not sure of the words she was biting back. Would the jumble in her head have emerged as a defence or apology?

Maya turned back to her stirring. 'Want some breakfast, Dante?' she asked, still not looking at him.

'No, he doesn't,' Beatrice said before Dante could respond. 'He was just going.' To emphasise the point she went to the door and opened it. The waft of cold, fresh, snowy air made her gasp but she stood her ground, appeal mingled with the determination in the glance she sent to Dante.

'Nice to see you, Maya.' The petite figure continued to stir, presenting her back to him, but he could feel the disapproval radiating off her in waves.

The door closed; the tension left Beatrice's body. She grabbed the back of one of the dining chairs and lowered herself into the modern plastic bucket seat. 'How's your head? The migraine gone?'

'Fine. All I needed was an early night, but it seems that things got interesting after I left.' Maya took her pan off the stove and poured a coffee from the full pot. She placed it on the table in front of Beatrice, a worried frown puckering her brow as she scanned her sister's face.

Beatrice cleared her throat. 'You must be wondering.' Now there was an understatement.

Maya shook her head. 'Just tell me you're not getting back together, you're not going back to San Macizo…'

'I'm never seeing him again,' Beatrice said and burst into tears.

As for San Macizo, the last time she had left she had left behind part of herself. If she went back she knew she'd lose what she had left.

'Thank God!' Maya hefted out a deep sigh of relief.

Beatrice sniffed and dashed the moisture from her face with the back of her hand.

'Oh, I know it's not my…and I'm *trying* to be objective, but honestly, when you came back last time looking like a…a…'

Shocked by the expression on her sister's face, Beatrice covered her small hand with her own. 'I'm not going back,' she cut in, holding her sister's teary, scared gaze.

'So what was he…?'

'Reynard has had a stroke.'

Dismay spread across Maya's heart-shaped face, melting away the last wisps of disapproval. 'Oh, I'm so sorry. Reynard was such a lovely man, with such a wicked sense of humour. When is the funeral? I'd like to come if I may?'

'It wasn't fatal,' Beatrice said quickly. She got up, picked up a piece of toast and started to butter it, not because she could have eaten a bite, just for something to do. 'So those buyers lined up to view the samples…'

'Changing the subject, Bea?'

'I know you don't like Dante.'

'I think Dante is perfectly charming,' Maya inserted, her lips curving into a wry smile, before adding, 'But I don't, I can't, *like* anyone who makes you unhappy.'

'I'm not unhappy.'

It was an obvious struggle for Maya not to challenge this statement, but lip-biting won out.

'And Dante is gone. He's never coming back.'

This time the crying went on a long time.

CHAPTER FIVE

'*DATES!*'

Beatrice blinked, caught between confusion and panic. She dragged her wandering blue gaze back to the young GP's face and allowed the professional encouraging smile to drag her back from the brink of panic. Though kick-starting her brain remained a non-starter—she felt utterly incapable of forming coherent thoughts.

'Dates…?' she echoed, as though she were thinking about it, which she wasn't. Thinking was simply not an option.

The reality was she could barely remember her name, let alone the information the locum GP, a young woman her own age, was asking for. Her regular doctor was, ironically, given the circumstances, on paternity leave.

'I know… I think…' She clenched her hands as she struggled to push past the loud static buzz in her head, which she explained by telling herself she needed a sugar hit. She hadn't managed to keep her breakfast down or, for that matter, last night's supper...*again*!

'Take your time,' the woman said, even though Beatrice was sure she had overrun her allowed time slot by a long way. An image of the foot-tapping disapproval as fellow patients glanced at the clock on the waiting-room wall flashed into her head—she'd been there, done that herself.

This doctor, with the relaxed attitude to time, seemed nice and sympathetic, which might not be a good thing. She had reached the point where it would only take a kind word to release the tears she could feel pressing against her eyelids.

So Beatrice avoided the sympathy and focused on the hole in the woman's tights as she wrapped her arms around herself in a self-protective hug to combat the cold inside her that was making her teeth chatter and sending intermittent tremors through her body.

'So, I'm assuming that this wasn't planned?' the medic, who had scooted her chair around to Beatrice's side of the desk, suggested.

Beatrice shook her head and wished the medic's calm were contagious, but then the professional had seen this a hundred times before and this wasn't professional for Beatrice.

'Statistically pregnancies rarely are planned.'

Tell me about it, she thought, swallowing the ironic laugh locked in her aching throat. 'Really?' If that was meant to make her feel better, it didn't.

'Did someone come with you?'

Beatrice reeled in her wandering thoughts, back from the unknown and scary future they had drifted towards, and tried very hard to focus on the here and now and not fainting—she *never* fainted.

'Someone...?' She moved her head, a tiny jerky, shaking motion, before clearing her throat, relieved when she responded with a close approximation of someone who had not totally lost it. 'Yes...yes, my sister.'

Who had refused to take no for an answer and had tagged along to the appointment that Beatrice had made after the stomach bug had not cleared up. Had Maya sussed the truth... had she?

Of course she had, but she'd buried the knowledge so deep...constructed so many perfectly reasonable, safe alternatives that it had not lessened the mind-deadening shock when confronted with the inevitable reality.

Despite the shock, her body continued to perform all its automated responses: she was breathing and moving, putting one foot... Actually she wasn't—she was sitting down and her knees were shaking. She was thinking, *Well, maybe not.* Her thoughts continued to refuse to move beyond the big mental brick wall. *I am pregnant.*

In her head she tacked several large exclamation marks on the acknowledgement, which did not make it feel any more real.

'I'm six weeks,' she said suddenly, her tone making it clear there were no ifs and buts or maybes about this. A warmth heated her pale cheeks as her thoughts drifted back to the night she'd spent under the duvet in the ski lodge with Dante. Sometimes on top of the duvet and sometimes... She felt a shameful flash of heat and closed down the thought of the night they had made a baby. 'It's our eighteen-month anniversary today...'

'Congratulations. Your husband isn't here today?'

Beatrice watched the doctor tap some keys on the computer and grimace as she noticed the hole in her tights.

'He's out of the country,' she said carefully.

'Would you like me to...? Shall I ask your sister to come in?'

Beatrice gave a pale smile of gratitude. 'Yes, please.'

* * *

A short while later she and Maya were out of the surgery and back in the fresh air. Beatrice expelled a long shuddering sigh and squeezed her eyes closed, opening them as she felt Maya's arm link with her own.

'Fancy walking back through the park?'

'Didn't we drive here?' If she had imagined that she was in even worse shape than she thought, Beatrice decided.

'Yes, but the fresh air might do us good… I'll pick up the car later.' She glanced at the little vintage car they had jointly bought when they first set up home together. It had seen better days.

Beatrice shrugged. 'Why not?'

The watery spring sun had come out from behind the clouds as they trudged beneath the skeletal branches of a row of poplars and past the snowdrops that were pushing up through the cold ground.

It was Maya who broke the silence.

'I love the smell of spring, all that promise of new life…' She pulled her wandering gaze, which had drifted to her sister's flat stomach, upwards. 'Sorry, I didn't mean to be profound or anything.'

Beatrice turned her head, then, as her eyes connected with the concern clouding Maya's eyes that her sister was unable to hide, she quickly looked away. 'You knew?' she asked, digging her hands into the deep pockets of her coat.

'It seemed…a…possibility…'

'You must think I'm a total idiot!' So must the doctor, not that she could remember the things she had said or any details of her own responses.

'I will think you're an idiot if you carry on saying daft things like that.'

Beatrice produced a pale, lacklustre smile in response. 'I suppose I must have known,' she admitted, thinking of all the signs that had been there. 'But I didn't think it would happen again…after…' Her voice trailed away, a faint ironic smile tugging at the corners of her lips as her thoughts drifted to the words of unbidden advice Dante's grandfather, still autocratically regal despite the fact he had passed on his official title to his son after a stroke, had offered. *Relax, woman.*

His words had stuck in her mind, mainly because at the time everyone else had been telling her to panic, if not in so many words—it had not been hard to read between the lines or the glances and conversations that halted abruptly when she appeared.

Well, it turned out that old Reynard was

right all along. All she had needed to do was relax…

Oh, God, no one had ever accused her of having good timing.

Beatrice turned her head. The worried expression on her sister's face pushed her into speech. 'It's just everyone was waiting, every month…and letting myself hope, and then having to tell Dante when it didn't happen.' He had acted as though it didn't matter, but she knew it did; she knew that as far as the palace was concerned her fertility had stopped being a private matter the moment Dante became Crown Prince.

She looked down at her flat belly and tried to separate the confusing mess of conflicting emotions fighting for supremacy in her head. 'A year ago, this would have made him so happy.' Frowning, she worried her full lower lip and wondered about his reaction now. Who was she kidding? She knew *exactly* what his reaction would be when he discovered that she was carrying the heir to the throne.

This was the end of her new life; there was no way he would allow her to bring up his child outside San Macizo.

'Is that why you left…?'

'Left?' Beatrice gave a vague shake of her head.

Maya studied her sister's face and glanced around for a convenient park bench, hoping they would make it there before Beatrice folded.

'You never said *why*, just that it was over, when you got home.'

Beatrice gave a sad smile. 'I'm pretty sure that it was why Dante made it easy for me to go.'

Maya caught her hand as Beatrice's voice became suspended by tears.

'You never asked me before,' Beatrice said.

'I thought you'd tell me when you were ready.'

'It's hard to explain my life. I felt like I'd stepped into a trickling stream and ended up trying to keep my head above raging white water. Things happened so fast—one minute I was me and the next I was pregnant and married.'

'Then you were a princess.'

Beatrice forced a laugh. 'A very bad one... then I lost the baby and there was no time to grieve.' She compressed her quivering lips. 'I was expected to do my duty and provide an heir. People acted as though our first baby had never existed. I hate now that I kept apologising, when I wanted—' She had wanted to hear Dante say that she didn't have anything to apologise for, that a baby shouldn't be about duty, it should be about *love*.

But he hadn't.

But then love had not been a word her husband had ever used. *Did he even believe it existed?*

He had been happy to tell her how much he *wanted* her, his throaty voice making her insides dissolve. But even then, sometimes she'd got the impression that he'd given in to the desire she awoke in him reluctantly.

She had told herself that discussing feelings was hard for some men, but beneath the rationalising she had known it was more than that.

She couldn't acknowledge her secret fear that the issue wasn't his inability to acknowledge his deep feelings; no, she worried that he just didn't have them. After the baby was gone, there was nothing deep connecting them, just passion... And now there was another life.

She gave a bleak little laugh and turned to Maya. 'I wonder if there are any statistics about the rate of divorce for Vegas marriages?'

'You sure there is going to be a divorce now?'

Beatrice decided not to acknowledge the

doubt she could see in her sister's eyes. It was a doubt she shared, a doubt she was trying very hard not to confront.

'I think you need to sit down,' Maya added, stepping off the pathway and approaching a bench.

It took Beatrice a few moments before she roused herself enough to react to the prompt of her sister patting the seat beside her.

Hunched forward, Beatrice planted her hands on juddering knees.

Maya put one small hand onto one of hers. 'Tell me to shut up, it's none of my business, but what happened, Bea?'

'I found it pencilled into my diary.'

'What?'

'An appointment with an IVF specialist,' she said. Maya was the only one who would know the full significance of that.

Her sister did. 'Oh, my God, what did you do?'

'Other than not be like Mum, you mean? Oh, you know me, very subtle and royal to my fingertips. I charged into Dante's meeting with a room full of the island's captains of industry and told him that enough was enough. That I didn't want staff, I didn't want a diary and that my childbearing hips were not a subject for staff meetings!'

She remembered the white line of fury out-lining his sensual lips as he had escorted her from the room.

Beatrice shrugged, her eyes following the antics of a squirrel that was running through the branches of a nearby tree.

'He called me naive and said I was over-reacting.' The lingering bitterness hardened her voice. 'I probably was, and, oh…it's hard to describe what it's like in the palace.' She lifted her hands, her long fingers slid-ing through her silky blonde hair, lifting the tangled strands off her neck before she let it fall in silky waves down her back.

'I wanted to wait. I didn't want a baby then. I was still grieving for the one I'd lost… Oh, I know they were only a bundle of cells, but—'

'Of course you needed time. Didn't Dante understand how you felt?'

'I never told him. We didn't discuss it…or actually anything much. With Carl gone, he was under a lot of pressure. Maybe I'm more like Mum than I thought,' she mused, remem-bering her words of moments ago—it would have made *him* happy.

When did she stop asking herself what would make her happy?

Like her own mother, she had seen what

she wanted to; she had put her own needs to one side to please a man.

'Oh, Bea, you know that's not true!'

Beatrice's glance fluttered from her sister's face across the flash of cheery yellow where winter jasmine was in bloom.

'I'm going to have a baby.' She said it like a practice run, imaging herself throwing the line into the conversation, but no, her imagination fell short. It still didn't feel real. 'I really do have great timing, don't I?'

'I wouldn't say the timing is just down to you,' her sister responded drily.

'I will have to tell Dante.'

Maya's expression softened into sympathy as she saw the realisation hit home for Beatrice, who began to scrabble for her phone in the bag that was looped across her shoulder.

'Give yourself time first, to get your own head around it,' Maya advised, trying to hide the worry she felt behind an encouraging smile.

Beatrice, her teeth worrying at her full lower lip, shook her head. The way she felt right now, that moment might never come and the longer she left it—well, it was never going to get any easier.

'Do I have to tell him?' she said with a surge of wild hope that vanished into guilt as she connected with the sympathy in her sister's eyes. 'I didn't mean that. It's just that everything will change. This baby is second in line to the throne.' It seemed like a terrible responsibility to give a child before they were even born. 'Dante had a bad childhood, you know, and now this baby will be brought up in that world…'

'Dante had a bad childhood because his parents are vile self-centred narcissists. This baby will have you.'

'If I go back.' In her heart she knew there was no *if* about it. The baby made it a forgone conclusion. 'It won't be like the last time. I won't be brought out like some sort of—'

'Don't tell me, Bea,' Maya cut in. 'Tell him. Did he know about Mum and the IVF thing?'

Beatrice shook her head. 'It seems like yesterday sometimes.'

The sisters' eyes met, their glances holding as they both remembered the period in their teens when, in an attempt to satisfy her husband's demands for a child of their own, their mother had turned to IVF to give him the *real* child he had wanted, which he had said would make them a *real* family.

Witnessing the physical and mental toll that cycle after cycle of treatment had wrought on their mother's health had been bad, but what had been worse was the blame game that had come after each failure from the man who held his wife responsible for not providing him with his *own* child.

'*Do you have any idea what this is doing to me?*'

The familiar petulant response had soon set the tone of their stepfather's reaction to having *his* plans disappointed. It had always been *her* fault: if she had *rested* more, if she had been more motivated, healthier, thinner, fatter…*if…if…* The list of accusations had been endless.

When one specialist had refused to treat them any more because of the impact on their mother's health, they had moved on to the next clinic.

'I used to think that I'd never go down that road…' Maya said suddenly. 'But, do you remember Prue?'

'The Prue who married the cricket player, but is much more famous for doing your maths homework?'

'She and Jake had twins through IVF. I've never seen two people happier.'

'That's not the same. Prue and her cricketer wanted a baby because they loved…' Beatrice felt her eyes fill. 'It wasn't duty. I left of my own volition, but it was only a matter of time before Dante would have been forced to put me aside for someone with a more reliable reproductive system.'

'He is a total bastard,' Maya said conversationally.

'He's the father of my child.'

Maya grimaced. 'I'm sorry…'

'I'm not.' Beatrice pressed her hands to her still-flat stomach. The panic was still there but it was pushed into the background by a certainty. 'You probably think I'm mad, but I *want* this baby.'

Maya smiled. 'I don't think you're mad, I think you're… I think you'll make a marvellous mum and I intend to be a pretty great auntie too.' Her eyes widened with awed realisation. 'God, with you as a mum and Dante as a dad, this baby really has hit the gene jackpot.'

CHAPTER SIX

'I'M AFRAID HIS Highness is—'

'Unavailable at the moment?' Beatrice inserted, her words dripping with saccharine-coated sarcastic venom, not caring by this point that she was killing the messenger.

This messenger at least.

It had taken all her courage to make that first call and she had felt physically sick as she had punched in Dante's personal number, only to have her call diverted to someone who had identified herself as 'His *Royal* Highness the Crown Prince's office'—not actually an office but a snooty-sounding female, whom Beatrice took an instant dislike to.

Over the last few hours her instincts had proved to be bang on. She also knew that her husband was ghosting her—every single number or email address she had for him came up as unrecognised or no longer available.

The only number that was taking her calls was this one.

'His *Royal* Highness is not taking calls but I can pass on a message.'

'Yes, you mentioned that,' Beatrice cut her off before she went deep into auto message mode.

This was the fifth time now that she had tried to contact Dante and the fifth time she had been given the same runaround by this faceless underling with the nice line in patronising.

'But if you would prefer to address your questions to His Highness's legal representatives… Do you have the number of the law firm? I can—'

Eyes squeezed tight, Beatrice told her exactly what she could do, and heard the shocked, offended gasp on the other end. She wasn't proud of it, but there were limits, and she had reached hers and then some.

In the periphery of her vision she was aware of Maya's frantic hand signals as she mimed zipping motions across her lips.

She ignored them and smiled. She wasn't enjoying herself, but it was a relief to stick her head over the parapet and stick it to Dante's messenger.

'I don't actually have any *questions*, I just want to deliver some information.'

'I will pass on any important information.'

'It is personal information. Sensitive information.'

'I am a *personal* assistant.'

'In that case…why not?' Beatrice came back smoothly. 'Do you have a pen? Fine, yes, well, take this down, will you? Tell my *husband*…' She ground the title home as she jabbed the pencil she had picked up into the stack of unopened post on the table. 'Tell him that I thought he might like to know that he is going to be a father. Got that?' she asked pleasantly, and decided to take the choked sound at the other end of the line as an affirmative. 'Well, thank you so much for your help. I'll be sure to mention your name when I speak to my husband!' Her breath gusting fast and frantic, she ended the call, her glance moving from the phone, still grasped in her white-knuckled hand, to her sister.

She pressed her hand to her mouth and gave a nervous giggle, her eyes flying to Maya, who rolled her own.

'You didn't stick to your script.'

'No, I didn't.' Beatrice looked at the stack of bullet points printed on cards that had been meant to aid her calm delivery of the facts, even factoring in a potential mind blank when it came to telling Dante.

She had not factored in a red-mist moment.

'I imagine you might get a response now,' Maya murmured as Beatrice continued to look at the phone in her hand as if it were an unexploded bomb.

'I lost my temper. What have I done now?'

It had been three in the morning before Beatrice had finally managed to drop off, so it took her a few moments to orientate herself and realise that the noise was not part of her dream, but real.

Someone—it didn't take too many guesses who—had their hand pressed to the doorbell, filling the flat with a continual tiny rendition of the 'William Tell Overture', their landlord's tasteful choice.

Maya appeared as Bea was dragging on a robe over her nightshirt.

'How did he get here this quickly?'

Beatrice shrugged.

'Shall I get it, tell him to come back later?'

'Like that's going to work…' She dragged a hand through her tousled hair and tried to dredge up some calm. 'No…no, I'll be fine.' She took another deep breath, and tightened the sash on her full-length robe as she lifted her chin to a defiant angle.

Maya looked doubtful. 'If you say so. I'll be in my bedroom if you need me.'

'Thanks.' Beatrice smiled but barely noticed her sister go; her thoughts had already moved on to the person outside the door.

She was vaguely conscious of her sister's bedroom door clicking closed as she blew out a slow calming breath, which didn't slow the speed of her pounding heart even a little, and reached for the handle.

Leaving the safety catch in place, she opened it. The action would normally have revealed the communal hallway, with a worn rug that covered the scratched parquet floor, and a noticeboard. But today all she could see through the door was Dante, who effectively blocked everything else from view.

He pushed himself off the wall and far enough away for her to see more of the dark suit he was wearing. Not his normal immaculate self—the fabric was crumpled and his white shirt was open at the neck, revealing a section of warm brown skin—but she barely noticed these details. All she saw, or rather felt, were the powerful, raw emotions that were emanating from him.

'You moved.' Dante had been keeping his

emotions in check, but the sight of her standing there and he could feel them slipping through his fingers like a wet rope, taking his control with it. 'No one told me.'

The journey here—he'd been mid-Atlantic when he had received the message, a sentence that was going to literally change his life in ways he was still too shocked to imagine—had already pushed his control to the limits.

The sight of her big blue eyes looking warily at him through the gap, rimmed with red from where she had been crying, didn't make him any less furious. It just added another layer to the emotions fighting for supremacy in his chest.

'Last week—it's bigger.' Just as she would be soon. An idea that still seemed deeply strange and not quite *real*.

Dante was very real though, and *very* angry.

'The people who live there now seem… I left my security team persuading them I am not dangerous.' While he had spent several frustrating minutes finding the correct address to give his driver.

'What are you doing here?' The accusing words floated through the gap and drew a low feral disbelieving growl from his throat.

'Are you *serious*?'

'It really wasn't necessary for you to come in person. A simple acknowledgement you'd got the news would have done fine.'

'Well, I am here.'

'I'm sure everyone in the building knows that. Come back tomorrow.'

Was he meant to care what people thought?

'That isn't going to happen and we both know it. Are you going to let me in or would you like to have this discussion here?' He bestowed a scathing glance at his surroundings before fixing her with a steely bitter stare. 'Sorry, I forgot my megaphone, but I have several paparazzi on speed dial…if that is your preference? Sure, let's share the news! Oh, I forgot, you already have.' It would be interesting to know just how many people she had told before she had told him…but then he was only the father.

Her lips tightened at the sarcasm. 'Lower your voice and don't be so unreasonable.'

'I suppose I should consider myself lucky you didn't send the news by text!'

Although on second thoughts, he decided as he experienced a stomach-clenching chilled aftershock of what he had felt as he had listened to his stand-in PA tell him he was going to be a father, a text might have been preferable!

She slipped the safety chain and hastily backed away, standing there, arms folded across her chest, as he entered a hallway that had been described in the rental details as a spacious dining hall.

A slight exaggeration, but it had never felt this claustrophobically cramped before.

'I tried to contact you.'

'You didn't try very hard.'

Her lips compressed. 'I suppose it depends on your definition of hard. The number I have for you no longer exists. Though why I'm telling you this I don't know, because I assume that you're the one who arranged for my calls to be diverted to your robotic PA.'

'She's a very good PA.' And he might have sacked her, he realised, a furrow forming between his dark brows as he replayed the in-flight exchange.

The details of the incident were a little sketchy, but in his shocked state of mind he presumed he must have asked her to repeat what she had just said, because she had repeated, word for word, the message that had left him literally rigid with shock.

The second time of telling had involved the same words, but no longer a statement, more a question conveying a snide implication that he had taken exception to.

'*She* says *she is pregnant? Are you calling my wife a liar?*'

'She is very efficient,' he said now.

'Oh, I have no doubt that she was only saying what she was told to. I assume that it was you who told her that any further communication would be through our legal teams.'

'That,' he reminded her grimly, 'was your idea.'

'I should have known it would be my fault.' Without warning the fight drained out of her, leaving her feeling weak-kneed, shaky and fighting back tears.

'Are you all right?'

She scraped together enough defiance to throw back a querulous, 'I'm pregnant, not ill.'

His chest lifted in a silent sigh. 'So, it's true?'

'Obviously not. I just made it up.'

'Sorry, that was a stupid thing to say.'

She squeezed her eyes closed and felt his hand on her elbow. 'Yes, it was.' She opened her eyes and shook her head, unable to keep a quiver of emotion out of her voice as she tilted her head back to look him in the face.

'You should sit down.'

'I should be in bed. I *was* in bed.' Conscious of her shaky knees and the fact she was grateful for the support of his hand, she nodded to the door just behind him. 'The sitting room is through there,' she said, afraid that he might take the next door, to her bedroom. Bedrooms were where all this had started. 'Be careful. There are boxes we haven't got around to unpacking yet.'

Skirting the packing cases, he continued to hover protectively until she had sat down on one of the sofas.

'So, have you seen a doctor?' he asked, dropping into a squat beside her. He scanned her pale features and felt a gut punch of guilt. She looked as if she had been crying for a week. Maybe she had. She looked so fragile that he was afraid to hold her. She looked as if she might break.

She nodded.

'So, there's no mistake.' Under the fresh wave of guilt he was conscious of something new. A possessiveness, a protectiveness.

She shook her head, feeling tears threaten again as she wondered if that was what he had been hoping. That this was all some mistake that they would laugh about. She couldn't really blame him.

'And a scan?'

'Not yet…what are you doing?'

He lifted the phone away from his ear. 'Making arrangements.'

'Dante, it's half three in the morning.'

He shook his head as though the relevance passed him by.

'I know in your world you can demand anything you want at any time of day and people will jump, but in my world we make appointments in daylight hours and get put on waiting lists.'

'*Waiting* lists?'

'If you want to do something, make me a cup of tea. Ginger. It helps the nausea. The kitchen's through that way.' She tipped her head in the direction of an arch at the end of the room that fed into the galley kitchen. 'Teas are in the bottom cupboard, first right.'

She closed her eyes, pretty much too exhausted to see if he reacted and definitely too exhausted to argue. She didn't open them until she felt a hand on her arm.

'Drink,' he said, watching her.

She did, blowing on the surface of the liquid first to cool it as he took a seat on the opposite sofa. He appeared lost in his own thoughts.

Feeling like someone sitting in the eye of a storm, knowing that any second all hell would break loose again, she drank and felt a little less wretched.

She set her mug down on a side table and waited, tensing when Dante unfolded his long, lean length and got to his feet.

'I didn't think about the time,' he admitted. 'I was—'

'In shock—I know.'

'I realise that you must feel… I know this isn't what you wanted, but it is happening, and we have to deal with it.'

'We don't need to deal with anything.' She still felt as if she had been run over by a truck, but the tea was making her slightly more coherent. 'I am already *dealing*,' she added, anxious to correct any impression to the contrary she might have given. 'I'm booked in for my first scan, just to confirm dates, I think, in a few weeks.'

'Right, I'll cancel and have them schedule one for when we get back,' he murmured half to himself.

'*Back?*' she said, pretending a bewilderment she wasn't feeling as a cold fist tightened in her stomach.

'I'm not going anywhere. I'm here and I'm staying here.' She drew her knees up to her chest and wrapped her arms around them.

'Relax, once the divorce comes through we can sort out the details, how things will work.'

'What the hell are you talking about?' he ground out, realising that his life had changed the moment he had met Beatrice. Nothing had been the same since that day.

'There isn't going to be a divorce now you are carrying my child.'

She looked into his eyes and saw the same steely conviction that his voice carried. She half rose and subsided, shaking as panic spilled through her body.

She looked up at him, eyes looking even bigger. The dark rings around them making him think of a trapped animal.

'You are carrying our child, the heir to the throne. That changes everything.'

'He…she won't want that,' she said, pressing a hand to her stomach, the gesture unconscious.

'Shouldn't that be their call? Are you going to try and rob that child of their heritage, their birthright?'

'It didn't make you or Carl very happy,' she slung back.

'We don't have to repeat the mistakes of my parents.'

She lifted a shaking hand to her head. 'There has to be another way. I can't go back to *that*…' She shook her head. 'I won't be manipulated and managed.'

He was looking at her with the strangest expression. 'Is that how you felt?'

His shock seemed genuine.

'It is the way it was.'

'It won't be like that when you go back. There will be changes.'

She didn't have the strength to hide her extreme scepticism even if she had wanted to. 'What changes?'

'To hell with opinion polls, I'm putting my family first. This is not about having an heir. It is about being a father.' Until this moment he had never appreciated the massive difference between the two. 'We'll make it work.'

'For the baby.'

He said nothing, the steely determination she saw shining in his eyes said it all as he took her chin between his fingers.

'You can't bring this child up alone…'

She fought the urge to turn her cheek into his palm. 'People do every day, some out of choice, some because there is no alternative.'

'But you *have* an alternative,' he cut in smoothly. 'We've had a trial separation, why not a trial marriage?'

'Another word for a sham? Been there, done that,' she said tiredly. The emotional and physical stress of the past days, and maybe the pregnancy hormones, were making their strength-sapping presence felt and her fight was being replaced by a dangerous fatalism.

Perhaps sensing her defences were failing, he leaned in towards her, bringing their faces level; she met his eyes and felt guilty for doubting his sincerity. There was nothing sham about the emotions rolling off him.

When she thought about it later, she decided it was the emotion in his face, the concern and self-recrimination that made her stop fighting the inevitable.

She lifted her chin. 'Things will *have* to change...if I come back,' she tacked on quickly.

'I promise there will be no *managing*.'

'I want to be more than a decorative accessory; I want to be treated as an equal, not patronised. Oh...' Her head dropped a little as she looked at him through the veil of her dark lashes. 'I don't want you to tell anyone, not until I'm three months along and things are...*safer*.'

'My parents?'

She gave a tiny laugh that left her blue eyes sombre. '*Especially* your parents.' She did not think she could stand any of their insincerity. They wanted a royal baby and for a while she'd be flavour of the month, but she knew that before long they'd be planning behind the scenes how to detach her from the baby.

Did the conviction make her paranoid? Well, better that than naive.

'They don't like me, they never liked me... which is fine, because I don't like them either.'

After a moment, he nodded. 'This waiting, secrecy...did the doctor indicate that anything was amiss? That there is a potential problem with this pregnancy, with you?' The tautness in him rose visibly as his sharpened glance moved across her face.

'No, it's just early, and if anything did happen like before...' She felt the tears form in her eyes and looked away, the muscles in her pale slender throat working as she fought to contain her fears. 'I don't want anyone else to know. I don't care what you tell them, just—'

Dante dropped the hand that lay curved around her cheek and, rising to his feet, stepped back. The ferocious surge of protectiveness he was experiencing as he watched her was less easy to step away from.

'Nothing will happen.'

'You can't say that,' she choked back, looking at him through glistening blue eyes. 'Because it does, for some people, over and over and—' Her voice cracked as she swallowed and felt a big fat tear trickle down her face as she felt his hand slide to the back of her head. 'I really don't think I could bear that,' she whispered, her voice muffled against his chest.

Helplessness and a fierce wave of protectiveness arched through him as he pressed a kiss to the top of her silky head and stroked her hair as she wept out her fear.

The sobs that shook her subsided but she allowed herself a few moments of lying there, taking comfort from the solidity of his chest, the strength of his arms, finally heaving a deep sigh as she pulled free.

'Thank you,' she said with a loud sniff.

Dante felt something nameless twist hard inside him as he rose from the kneeling position he had fallen to beside the sofa. 'You are welcome.'

'I must look terrible.'

'Horrific. That's better,' he approved as she gave a watery smile. 'And soon you will get fat and you won't be able to see your feet.'

Will you still love me?

The words stayed in her head because he didn't love her now.

CHAPTER SEVEN

THEY EMERGED FROM the low-lying fog that had blanketed the area around the private airport into the spirit-lifting blue above. Beatrice's spirits didn't lift; the nervous tension making her shoulders ache didn't dissipate as she undid her seat belt and leaned back in the seat that bore an imprint of the Velazquez crown on the leather headrest. It had more of a welcoming embrace than any she had received from the Velazquez family, but then they were not really a *tactile* family.

She was under no illusions that any welcome she had in the future would be because of the baby. She didn't care about that, but the equally inescapable fact was that Dante only wanted her here because of the baby. She avoided the temptation to read anything else into his determination to rekindle their marriage.

The pilot's disembodied voice spoke, adding to his words of welcome the less welcome fact that there was the possibility of some turbulence ahead. *Tell me about it*, Beatrice thought, looking around and seeing that someone had already whisked away the fur-lined parka coat she had worn for the journey to the airport. She wouldn't need it, or the layers she had on underneath, at the other end. San Macizo enjoyed an all-year-round temperate climate.

She continued to exchange her boots for the flats she had pushed into her bag as Dante translated the pilot's Italian words.

She smiled and nodded absently, even though she hadn't needed him to translate. She had continued the lessons she had begun without much optimism during her brief sojourn in San Macizo where Italian, introduced to the country by the royal family centuries before, was the official language. Though she had never encountered a native who didn't speak English and French fluently, like Dante, who was also fluent in Arabic and Spanish.

Free of her layers, she adjusted the cuffs on her white shirt and watched as Dante unfastened his own seat belt and the buttons on his dark grey suit jacket and waited, wondering if it was worth getting the paperback out of her bag. She doubted she'd be able to concentrate—her nerves were too wound up.

No massive surprise there. What she had committed to was about as sane as deliberately opening a half-healed wound, and, as it turned out, just as painful. Up to the point of being welcomed onto the private jet she had not allowed herself to think about what lay ahead. Now she couldn't *stop* thinking about it.

After a few moments, a small frown appeared between her brows. Dante hadn't got up to seek a quiet, private office space to work in; he hadn't even reached for the laptop that lay on the seat next to him, let alone buried himself in it.

She found this break in familiar routine slightly unnerving. She searched her memory and could not remember a time, at least not since he had stepped into the role his brother had walked away from, that Dante hadn't immersed himself into work at every opportunity.

She had teased him at first about his ability to totally shut out distractions until she had realised that she was one of those distractions, then it had seemed less amusing.

Dante still showed no sign of moving away, and doing so herself would seem a bit obvious, so she exhaled a resigned sigh and reached for her book. Even if she could not lose herself in the world of fiction she would have somewhere to look that wasn't directly at her husband. *Husband...* She could remember saying that word out loud and smiling—it seemed a long time ago.

These days she felt impatient with her younger self for being so naive; while she had been walking on air she doubted that, despite what was written on a piece of paper, Dante had ever felt he was her husband, not really. But he *was* the father of her child.

She desperately wanted this baby. It was that utter certainty that was getting her through; the life growing inside her was light at the end of the tunnel.

She couldn't assume that Dante would feel the same way. She had to see things the way they were and not the way she wanted them to be.

Attracted to the wrong man and refusing to see the things that she didn't want to. *Now, where have I seen that before?* An image of her mother's face floated into her mind.

Beatrice found the idea of history repeating itself through the generations deeply depressing and she intended to break that cycle. It was just a pity she hadn't displayed the insight earlier, instead of spending her short marriage living in a fantasy world of her own making.

Just thinking about it, she could taste the self-disgust in her mouth. The irony was, of course, that when she had finally opened her eyes to the reality of her marriage it had been impossible not to be struck by the fact she had been guilty of the same weakness that she had struggled to forgive in her own mother.

But though she couldn't avoid the glaring comparison with her own mother, she had never extended it to include Dante, who was nothing like her ex-stepfather, who had been a manipulative, cruel bully with a sadistic streak.

Dante was not the man she had *wanted* him to be. She had created a fiction; that did not make him a bad person. He was absolutely straightforward, strong, complex, impatient, arrogant and had zero tolerance for incompetence, but his only real sin had only ever been not to be in love with her.

But that didn't mean she had the right to rob their child of a father's love, nor rob their child of his heritage. But she was equally determined not to allow that heritage to emotionally damage the baby.

'Are you all right?'

She jumped as the sound of Dante's voice broke into her thoughts.

'What? Yes. Why…?'

One sardonic brow hitched, he nodded towards the book on her lap. 'It's upside down.'

She felt the guilty flush climb up her neck as she turned it around and then closed it. 'I never liked flying much.'

'There are no barriers, medically speaking, for you to fly at this stage.' He caught her surprised look. 'I have been reading up a little.'

'This is staying between us for now… *right*?'

'I have made some enquiries concerning obstetricians. *Discreet* enquiries. I understand that early monitoring is important.'

She thought about that and nodded. 'So, what have you told your parents?'

'I have told them we are back together.'

'That must have gone down well!'

'They need not concern you. If it makes you feel any more relaxed about it, I stopped trying to please them a long time ago, about when I realised it was never going to happen.'

He remembered the exact moment. He had been watching the flames of an open fire lick the Christmas card he had made them. The Christmas card they hadn't even bothered to open.

By the time it had collapsed into a pile

of ashes he had decided that if they considered him the wild one, the unreliable one, the one who always caused them a headache, he might as well enjoy himself and do what people expected him to.

'Ah, I almost forgot. My grandfather sends his best wishes and says he hopes you can give him a decent game.'

Still wondering about his previous comments, she allowed herself a smile. 'At least I have one friend in the palace.'

Something flicked across his face that she struggled to interpret. 'You have a husband...'

Her glance fell. 'I haven't forgotten,' she said, thinking that it was a pity he couldn't say the same about her. The moment the palace doors had closed behind them she had been delegated out, the only use he'd had for her recreational.

'That was a big sigh... It is a steep learning curve, for me too.'

Surprised by the unexpected admission, she stared at him.

'Sadly, there are no intensive courses on being a Crown Prince. I had some valuable advice. My parents advised I delegate, which, as you might have noticed, is their management style. Grandfather, whose advice was actually quite helpful, said that I should trust no one and don't believe a word you're told.'

As he had hoped, his comment drew a laugh from Beatrice. The sound made him smile too, then his smile faded as he realised how much he had missed that sound.

'And now you have found your own style?'

'I like to think I have steered a personal course somewhere in between idle disregard for anything but my own comfort and paranoia, but the jury is out.'

As their smiling glances met and clung, she was aware of the perceptible shift in the atmosphere.

She pulled in a tense breath and looked away.

'Is something wrong? You can tell me.'

The unexpected addition brought her glance sweeping upwards. 'You just seem…?'

She paused, pulling in a long steadying breath, and wondered if the day would come when she could look at him and feel only aesthetic appreciation rather than an ache of need. You'd have thought that after a while boredom would have kicked in, but she could have happily stared at him forever.

'Seem?'

'Maybe it's just that you're—'

'I'm what?' he prompted with slightly less patience.

'It's that you're still...' Her hands moved in a descriptive sweep that made the collection of silver bracelets she wore on her left wrist jangle. 'You're here.'

His dark brows knitted; he looked genuinely mystified. 'Where else would I be?'

A small laugh burst from her lips. Had Dante *really* never realised that from the moment the news had been delivered that his brother had decided to renounce his claim to the throne, Dante had tuned her out, more than distance, much more than an understandable preoccupation with the role that had been thrust upon him?

She had felt at best surplus to requirements, at worst, an embarrassment.

'Busy with more important things?' she flung out and bit her lip as her unthinking retort was laden with an inch-thick layer of bitterness.

She lifted a hank of slippery, shiny hair that was crawling down the collar of her crisp white shirt, then catching the direction of his gaze made her glance towards the folded cashmere sweater she had discarded as she gritted her teeth and fought the ludicrous impulse to fasten another button, or pull her sweater back on. Instead she smoothed the non-existent creases in the tailored pale cream trousers and fussed with the buckle on the narrow red leather belt that held them up, just to give her hands something to do.

Her lips twisted as she noticed that Dante seemed to be having a similar problem. His long fingers flexed and clenched as if he was fighting an instinct to reach for his laptop after her comment.

She vented an internal sigh. Ah, well, this looked like it was going to be a nice relaxing journey—always supposing you were the sort of person who found nail-biting tension and sitting on the edge of your seat while looking for an escape route relaxing!

She adopted a carefully neutral expression as she lifted her chin and crossed her feet neatly at the ankle. The soft leather flats she had changed into proved you could look fashionable and be comfortable. Well, at least from the ankle down—being comfortable elsewhere was hard when she remained so acutely conscious of the restrained power Dante exuded. Always a challenge to cope with, but overpowering in any enclosed space, and right now her feelings were too raw and close to the surface to make her feel confident about disguising her vulnerability.

'I'm fine, feel free to…' She made an all-encompassing motion with her hand before she gave an elaborate yawn. 'I didn't get much sleep last night.'

She and Maya had talked into the small hours, and after her sister had gone to bed she had lain fully dressed on her bed staring at the ceiling, dreading the morning. She had finally fallen asleep half an hour before her phone alarm sounded, and had felt like death warmed up.

'Nor the night before,' she continued unthinkingly, then tacked on, 'That wasn't a dig.'

'I'm sorry I disturbed your sleep.'

'It wouldn't be the first time.'

The quiver of her stomach could have been connected with the lurch as they hit a pocket of turbulence, but she knew it wasn't.

'All right?'

'Fine. I always liked roller coasters.' She breathed through a wave of nausea and missed what he said next. 'Sorry…?' she pushed out, her hand pressed to her throat.

'I said…' He paused, his heavy-lidded glance lingering on the dark smudges beneath her glorious eyes.

Dante didn't know where he stood on the nature, nurture debate, whether he'd inherited the trait from his parents or simply learnt by example didn't seem the point, but whatever the truth he had always possessed the ability to step back and observe events and people from an objective perspective.

Except with Beatrice.

'You do look tired.'

'Thanks,' she murmured drily, translating the comment that he'd framed more like an accusation as, *You do look awful*.

'Maya and I were trying to decide what to do now that I'm, well…not there.'

'Setting up a business is challenging.' And he suspected that most of the work fell on Beatrice's shoulders. He had nothing against Maya, but she didn't seem that *dynamic*, and as far as he could tell she had a habit of not finishing things. From what Beatrice had let slip he had decided Maya was one of those people who were wildly enthusiastic, then lost enthusiasm when the project needed hard work.

Not the sort of person you'd choose to enter a partnership with.

'Is your sister intending to go it alone now?'

Beatrice felt a resurgence of her guilt. She was letting Maya down once more and her sister was being so damned nice about it, but they both agreed that she couldn't put her plans on hold again. 'She says she'd be happier to go for a less ambitious format.'

'You think she's lying.'

'Of course she is.'

He looked thoughtful. 'I was actually going to suggest that... I have some contacts—would she be open, do you think, to the idea of experts coming in to offer advice? And I know someone who might be interested in investing.'

'Someone, as in...you?'

'Someone anonymous,' he said smoothly.

'That is very generous of you.'

'It is in my best interests that you not spend your pregnancy worrying.'

'Well, I'll speak to her, but she can be a bit touchy. She has come up against a lot of prejudice, a lot of people who can't see past a young pretty face.'

'I wouldn't bet against either of you once you put your mind to something.'

Bea reacted with a glowing smile to the unexpected compliment; she couldn't help it, even though she knew his good opinion shouldn't matter. 'We like a challenge.'

He watched her smile fade.

'What is it?'

'I *want* to be a good mother.' Her eyes flickered wide in dismay. Standing in front of a

TV camera and confessing she was afraid she wasn't up to it would have been only *slightly* less embarrassing than revealing her insecurities this way.

'Then you will be.'

'You really think so?'

Before Dante could respond to her equally mortifying appeal for reassurance—her tongue seemed to have developed a will of its own—an attendant appeared.

Dante watched as the male attendant predictably went red and started stuttering when he spoke to Beatrice. He looked as if he was going to faint when she smiled encouragement.

Dante spoke sharply and the guy made an obvious effort to pull himself together, though his glance did keep straying to Beatrice.

While the young man waited, he turned to Beatrice. 'I ordered coffee and sandwiches, do you want some?'

Beatrice's smile held a hint of teasing triumph that he didn't understand until she turned to the young man and asked for tea and biscuits in halting but pretty good Italian.

Dante waited until the young man had vanished. 'So, when did that happen?'

She shrugged, and tried not to look complacent. 'I had a grounding. Even a not very good student can pick up quite a bit in ten months, so I carried on after I left. There are a lot of really great online courses available and some night classes at our local college. A second language is a useful skill.'

'That's a change of tune.'

'I'm doing the lessons now out of choice, not—'

His long fingers curled around his coffee cup as he raised it. 'You make it sound as though you were forced,' he said, looking at her over the rim.

'Forced? Maybe not,' she conceded. 'But I was definitely *not* consulted. Nobody asked if I wanted to have lessons.' It was only after she'd left and she'd found herself in an Italian restaurant that she had realised how much of what she had learnt had stuck. It was actually a shock to realise that she had learnt anything at all!

'And Maya has joined me, so we practise our conversational skills on each other... though Maya is much better than me. She's so much quicker than I am at picking up languages.'

He made a non-committal grunt that had her hackles rising. 'So now *you* don't believe *me*?' she challenged.

'Your sister has a gift for languages, fine,

if you say so.' He put down his coffee and leaned back, planting his interlaced fingers on the tabletop.

'I *do* say so.' She fixed him with a dangerous, narrow-eyed stare. 'Just what is your problem with my sister?'

'I don't have a problem…' he began and then stopped. 'All right, do you realise how much you sing her praises? It's constant. Maya is brilliant, Maya is beautiful, Maya says, Maya thinks,' he bit out. 'From what I understand Maya had all the same advantages as you but left school with virtually no qualifications, squeezed onto a degree course and then dropped out, worked for a charity, was it…? And yes…walked away…' He could feel his antagonism building. It was always *Maya's* birthday that deserved the special celebration, her crossing a road seemed to rate a hashtag, but it was Beatrice who was the powerhouse, the real talent!

'That was because…' Beatrice flared, then bit her lip. Maya was a private person and she respected that, even though she wanted to throw his assumptions in his face.

'Maya quits—*you* are the one with the exams, the degree, the successful career. Why do you defer to *her*?'

She reeled back, her hands gripping the

armrests, shocked by the sheer vehemence of his attack. 'I don't…' She stopped, her fluttering lashes framing the realisation that dawned in her deep blue eyes as she saw how her relationship with her sister might appear to him. 'You wouldn't understand.'

'Try me.'

Her desire to defend her sister outweighed her reluctance to confide details. 'I say those things…' She cleared the constriction in her throat. Her fists clenched, but so was everything inside too. 'I say those things, because for a long time nobody else did.'

His dark brows flattened into a line of confusion above his deep-set eyes as he shook his head. 'You're talking as if your sister is some sort of victim.' The petite brunette he knew had a core of steel under the delicate exterior. She was quiet, yes, but no shrinking violet. He judged it would take a very brave man to cross her or for that matter pierce the shell under the deceptively placid exterior.

'Not a victim, a *survivor*,' she bit back fiercely. Self-pity was not one of her sister's traits. 'You know our father died?' Beatrice had known then that their lives had changed, that nothing would be the same as it had been without his big warm presence, but she hadn't known how much it would change.

He nodded, wondering where this was going.

'And Mum made a second marriage.'

He nodded again. Rachel Monk had been divorced for some time when he had met her; it had been hard to tell what she would have been like under normal circumstances because the day they had met had not been *normal*. How did a mother respond when her daughter announced she had married a man the week before in Las Vegas and—cue drum roll—here he is?

He hadn't anticipated being welcomed into the bosom of the family, and he'd been prepared for worse than he'd got, but his own parents had more than made up for it. Luckily he'd been about ten when he'd last cared about their disapproval...or maybe that was when he'd started enjoying it.

After the initial shock, his new mother-in-law had been polite but not warm and on the handful of subsequent occasions they had met she had never relaxed in his company, continuing to view him as a threat to her daughter's happiness. She'd been proved right.

He remembered Beatrice mentioning the second marriage in passing, but she had not dwelt on the circumstances and he hadn't thought it warranted much curiosity in a world where very few marriages lasted long term, and those that did last, much as his parents', did not because they were happy, but because ending it would be too costly.

'They divorced years ago?'

'Yes, thank God!' There was nothing at all *in passing* about this emotional declaration.

'You didn't like him?'

'He was vile.' Beatrice aimed for statement of fact but it came out more hissing vehemence, which made it pointless to claim that time had done anything to lessen her feelings when it came to her stepfather.

Dante froze… His eyes went black; a chill slid down his spine. Suddenly it was hard to breathe. 'He *hurt* you?'

'Not me, no.'

The bunched aggression in his pumped muscles lowered fractionally, but the nerve beside his mouth continued to beat an erratic rhythm.

'He wasn't violent, he never raised a hand.' People always assumed that abuse was physical, but torture came in many forms. 'He didn't need to,' she said with quiet emphasis. 'And he never really bothered much about me. I was not his target. It turned out there are some inbuilt advantages in being too tall and gawky, which I was at that age.'

Dante's eyes swept across her face, taking in at once the soft, moulded contours of her smooth cheeks, the sensual curve of her full lips and her expressive cobalt blue eyes beneath the sweep of dark brows. It was hard to fit that face, those glorious supple curves, into an ugly duckling analogy. Impossible to imagine her anything other than jaw-droppingly beautiful.

But it might explain why she put so little store by her own beauty. Beatrice was the least vain woman he had ever met, with the most cause to be vain.

'He always liked to be the centre of attention, certainly Mum's attention, and he didn't like competition for it. He didn't consider me pretty or clever—people didn't smile when I walked into a room, unless I fell over my own feet.

'But he took against Maya from the start. She was so pretty, "like a doll" people would say—she actually hated that, she was a bit of a tomboy. And she was gifted—a precocious talent, they called it—and, you know, I think he sensed her bond with Mum… It was special.'

She paused, her blue eyes clouding with memories before she made a visible effort to compose herself.

'Mum and Dad always told her she was special because they didn't want her to feel second best when I came along. They wanted her to know that she was as much their real daughter as I was.'

'I had forgotten she was adopted.'

The description of the family dynamics brought his protective instincts to the surface. It seemed to him that it was inevitable the well-meaning parents had favoured their adopted daughter.

'What about you?'

She looked at him, startled, and shook her head.

'While Maya was being told she was special and enjoying her bond...?'

She gave a laugh and shook her head. 'No, I'm not explaining this very well.' Frustrated by her inability to describe the dynamics when they were growing up, she paused a moment before trying to explain. 'Mum and Dad wanted us to know we were *both* special, and the Maya and Mum thing...you can be loved by both parents but closer to one. I was a daddy's girl,' she admitted with sadness in her eyes. 'I was always closer to Dad than Mum.' He watched a shadow cross her face before she turned her head in a sharp negative gesture as though she was dislodging memories. 'We were just a happy family, even after Dad died. We had each other and then—'

He watched as she swallowed. She seemed unaware of her actions as she pressed a hand to the base of her throat.

'Everything changed almost overnight, but we clung together, and it was getting better. At first it was lovely to see Mum happier and getting dressed up. Maya and I would help her with her make-up before a date, and Edward was a charming man.

'Until they were married—he changed then. It was insidious, the way he cut Mum off from everything, everyone, including us. You didn't see it at the time and we were just kids. And he was careful to appear caring in front of Mum, but when she wasn't there, one of his weapons of choice against Maya was finding fault.' It sounded innocuous when she said it, but the cumulative effect had been devastating. 'He just chipped away at her on a daily basis. Nothing she did was good enough. He ridiculed her, laughed at anything she did and told her she was hopeless.'

In the end her sister had believed it.

Bea's eyes lifted from her determined contemplation of her clenched fingers in response to the harsh curses that Dante spat. They were not Italian words she was familiar with but she got the gist without a dictionary.

'He had a sadistic streak. He *wanted* to see her cry.'

Dante swore again, feeling the rage that a strong man felt for a bully. They called it coercive control; he called it being a pathetic coward. Lost in her memories, Beatrice didn't register it.

'And she tried so hard not to.' Beatrice brushed away the tears that had spilled from her eyes with an angry hand, recognising that there was an odd sense of relief that she was sharing things she had held close for years.

'She always had artistic talent. Early on, her teachers noticed it, encouraged it, and she is a brilliant artist. But Edward destroyed her confidence. He'd hold up her drawings and mock...' Her voice cracked at the painful memories that flooded her head. 'He made her feel useless. From a bright, bubbly girl she became withdrawn, but worse than all that was that Mum, when I told her, didn't believe me—not for a long time.' She sighed and looked at him, sadness behind her forced smile. 'So, you see, I do say Maya is brilliant a lot, because she is.'

'Yes, I see that.' It seemed to Dante that Maya was not the only *brilliant* Monk female.

Beatrice had been her sister's champion; there was no trace of envy in her and when he compared it with the resentment he had felt as a child, when he was pushed to the background with all the attention focused on his brother, the heir, he felt ashamed.

He felt a fresh kick of shame when he recalled how irritated he had felt about Beatrice's closeness to Maya, and his attitude when she became unreasonable, as he had seen it, at any hint of criticism of her sister.

Clearly the events of their childhood had created an unbreakable bond. If he had known, he wouldn't have wanted to break it, but he hadn't known, maybe because he had never asked. In fact, he had switched off when she'd spoken of her sister and not bothered to hide his lack of interest.

'I think the hardest part was feeling so helpless, but then I suppose I was meant to—it's all about power for creeps like Edward.'

As she stared out of the window it was almost as if she had forgotten he was there. She was saying things he wondered if she had ever said before. It was clear to Dante that Beatrice had not escaped as unscathed as she liked to think.

'Seeing what he did to Maya and then Mum, with the blasted IVF—he made her feel a failure too. Mum couldn't give him the family he wanted, his own family, and even though it was affecting her health he kept pushing her to try again and again. Telling her if she was a real wife, a proper wife, she wouldn't be sabotaging the attempts.'

His deep voice cursing jolted her free of the dark memories.

'Your mother had IVF?'

She nodded, and he swore. 'That is why you reacted to the consultation so...extremely. If I had known—'

'I don't think my reaction was extreme,' she rebutted, turning in her seat to face him. 'And, irrespective of my family history, I don't think something that personal, that intimate, should be delegated. It is something that is *discussed*.'

'I thought your reaction meant that you didn't really want children. That after the miscarriage, I assumed...'

Her hand went to her stomach, the gesture unconscious. 'I *knew* you didn't want children. You wanted an heir.'

He felt a flash of shame as he found himself thinking about the events in her life that had moulded Beatrice into the woman she was today.

He found this new experience unsettling,

as he considered this woman who didn't carry resentment. Her recount had focused on how her mother's ill-fated marriage had affected her sister, but the childhood trauma had to have impacted her too.

Men who hurt those in no position to hit back were one of the things in life that made Dante see red. He'd met them; they came in all guises, and he did everything within his power to make sure they did not flourish.

What he saw, and Beatrice did not, was that she had been a victim too, watching her sister and mother suffer and feeling helpless, going to a person who was meant to protect her and being disbelieved.

'Why didn't you tell me any of this?'

'It's not really my story, it's Maya's and…' She paused, her clear blue eyes meeting his with a directness that made him think she could read his shame. 'We never reached that point, did we? We were married, but really we were still two people dating.'

He looked about to say something, but he closed his mouth when she added quietly, 'And in the end, we skipped the bit of getting to know one another and went straight to divorce. We were on fast forward, all intense and…' She shook her head, suddenly overcome by emotion. He was there, a few feet away; all she had to do was reach out. The sheer craving inside her to seek the physical comfort of his strength was, for a split second, so overwhelming that she began to move towards him.

Then at the critical moment, the pilot's voice made her snap back.

'He's inviting me to...' Dante paused. 'You already know?'

'Go join him,' she said with encouraging brightness.

He half rose and subsided. 'No, it's fine.'

'I can cope for a few minutes without you.'

'I know you can—you have been for the last six months—but now you don't have to.'

CHAPTER EIGHT

BEATRICE TOOK SOME time freshening up. She reapplied some lipstick, smudged some more soft grey shadow on her eyelids and that was it—the recent exposure to the winter Alpine sun had given her skin a deep glow that made her look deceptively healthy, even though she felt tired and washed out.

Her freshly washed hair resisted her efforts to pull it back from her forehead and into a sleek ponytail on the nape of her neck, but she persevered and got a result that made her nod faint approval at her reflection.

A quick spritz of perfume before she shrugged on a long-line oversized blazer in a swirly print. She thought she might pass muster. Her lips curved into a small, reflective smile as she remembered the first time she'd stepped off one of the royal fleet of jets onto home tarmac. Except it hadn't felt like home as she knew it.

When Dante had said *private* she had assumed that this covered both the flight and the arrival—she'd been wrong! Stepping into the sun, she had found herself faced with a military guard of honour, several dignitaries and half the royal family, complete with hats and heels. She'd stepped out wearing jeans and a tee shirt emblazoned with a cartoon of a smiling monkey, and trainers that had seen better days. Her hair, waist-length, loose and wild.

Given the way she made her living, she was used to being the focus of attention, but that was playing a part. That day she hadn't had any fake sexy persona to hide behind—she had worn less in public but she had never felt more exposed.

She had been furious with Dante for not warning her, and he had added insult to injury by suggesting that she was overreacting.

She hadn't asked about today, but she was pretty sure that, given the circumstances, this would be low-key and not a hat-and-heels-and-handshakes occasion. But even if it had been, she no longer had anything to prove.

It was quite liberating to have already flunked the exams, and actually the intervening months had made her grow in confidence. Something that hadn't really hit home until now.

With a toss of her head that set her ponytail bobbing, she pushed up the sleeves on the oversized tailored blazer and went to join Dante. She tilted a smile up at him.

'So, let's do this.'

Dante had been scrolling through his phone as he'd waited. At the sound of her voice he slid it back into his pocket and turned his head. She sounded like a sports coach giving a confidence-boosting pep talk, but she looked like a goddess. He felt the heat flash down his front and settle painfully in his groin. Beatrice could make a sack look sexy; along with a perfect supple body, she had an innate sense of style.

He remembered the first time she'd arrived; the image would stay with him forever—Beatrice dressed in jeans that showed off her incredible bottom and endless legs, carrying off the military escort reception with a queenly confidence that had filled him with pride. She'd been mad as hell, he recalled, a reminiscent smile turning the corners of his mobile mouth upwards.

Beatrice felt the heat inside her rise as his dark gaze settled on her. She stood her ground and fought not to react.

'You look good.'

She tipped her head in acknowledgement; it hid the rush of blood that warmed her cheeks.

Their arrival was indeed low-key and, like the Italian lessons, it seemed she had learnt more than she'd thought. She nodded through the handshakes and smiles in a way she would once have thought unimaginable... Maybe it was because she had not had to impress anyone.

There was something quietly liberating about it. Was this the way Dante, who never tried to impress people, felt? She slid a glance at him as she stepped through the open door of the limousine. He was conversing with someone who had a serious expression and wore a holstered gun. She gave a little shiver. That was something she could never feel nostalgia for, along with bulletproof glass.

She had settled in her seat when the door opened, and Dante joined her. 'Sorry about that, just a message from Carl.'

She nodded but didn't ask. She was aware in the periphery of her vision that Dante was watching her.

'How is he?' she forced herself to ask.

She understood being close to a sibling, but she had never understood why Dante had never, ever displayed *any* resentment towards his older brother.

She had always been careful not to show how she felt but his next words suggested she hadn't been entirely successful.

'Our marriage problems were not down to Carl.'

'I don't think that,' she tossed back with a small unconvincing laugh. 'I never did.'

Strong marriages survived the storms, some were even made stronger, but theirs had sunk without trace at the first squall.

Why do you think it will be any different now?

She pushed away the doubts. 'What is the hold-up?' she gritted, bouncing out of her seat as she virtually pressed her nose to the window.

His eyes went from her foot tapping on the floor to the visible tension in her slim neck.

'This is going to work, you know.'

'Are you basing that on blind faith, or have you been reading the tea leaves again?' She stopped and grimaced, instantly ashamed of her outburst. 'Sorry. I… I'm a bit nervous about this.'

He reached out and curled his hand around hers, drawing it onto his lap. His action was so unexpected that for a moment all she could do was stare at his strong fingers, dark against her pale skin.

Her emotional reaction to his action was way over the top, she knew that, but she had no control over the tears that began to spill down her cheeks.

She pulled her hand free, mumbling, 'Hormones,' as she sniffed and dashed the moisture away with the back of her hand.

He could feel the tension rolling off her in waves; he felt a stab of guilt that his first reaction was to pretend he couldn't.

'Try and relax.'

She shot him a look; did he think this was easy? Perhaps he did, and why wouldn't he? In the past this was the point she would have nodded and hidden her nerves under a smile.

'This is me *trying*—I promise you.'

'You know what to expect this time.'

'That's the problem…' Panic closed her throat.

A wave of emotion moved through him as he watched her struggle, and he had no defence against the uncomfortable mixture of tenderness and guilt that stirred inside him as he looked into her beautiful unhappy eyes.

How many times had he made her unhappy?

Bea turned her head away, her thoughts

drifting back to Dante's comments about his brother. 'I like Carl.' Although Dante was right, there was a tiny part of her that did blame Carl.

Carl doesn't want to be King.

The sentence that had changed her life, but at the time it had elicited a muted but sympathetic response from her. She remembered thinking that she could not imagine what it was like to have your life mapped out from birth.

'I am supporting his decision.'

'His decision?'

'He is renouncing his title and his claim to the throne.'

Still she hadn't got what he was telling her. 'Is that even possible? What will he do?'

'Be happy.'

She had got a horrible feeling in her stomach at that moment that his happiness might come at a cost, and she'd been proved right.

She sighed, feeling petty and mean-spirited. She did not normally struggle with empathy, but when it came to the erstwhile Crown Prince he would be linked in her head forever with losing Dante on the heels of losing their baby. But then you couldn't lose what you'd never had.

'If it helps, I will be able to be there more than—'

Her glance swivelled his way, and she arched an enquiring brow.

'More than I was. There were a lot of people waiting for me to fail.' The admission seemed drawn from him almost against his will.

Beatrice stared. He had never said anything like that to her before. He sounded almost… *vulnerable*?

'We made this baby together, and we will make decisions about this baby together. I want to make this work.'

She swallowed. 'So do I.'

He nodded and sat back in his seat just as the convoy of armoured limousines, the metallic paint catching the sun, finally drove along a wide chestnut tree–lined boulevard that dissected the capital city of San Macizo. The strict development laws meant there were no skyscrapers to compete with the old historic buildings.

There were modern buildings, the glass fronts reflecting back images, but they blended in seamlessly with the old. Traces of the historic waves of invasion and occupation were everywhere. The eclectic mix extended to culture and food—the capital featured highly on international foodies' wish lists.

As they drove past the government building, Beatrice watched Dante's face as his eyes lifted to the national flag fluttering in the breeze. She wondered what he was thinking.

As they reached the high point on the road, the panoramic vista widened and Beatrice caught a glimpse of the sea through the dense pine forest that bordered the white sand on the eastern side of the island. The western coast was where the famed colonies of seabirds nested in the protected area around the high cliffs, drawing naturalists from around the world every breeding season, and giving inspiration for countless nature documentaries.

Beatrice had read all the guidebooks about the place that Dante called home before she'd arrived, but she had quickly realised that until you experienced the place you didn't really *get* just how dramatic the contrasts they spoke about were. It wasn't just the geography of the place. San Macizo had been conquered several times over the centuries, and each successive wave of invaders had brought their own culture and genes to the mix. There was no such thing as a *typical* San Macizan, but as you walked the streets of the capital it soon became obvious there was an above average quantity of good-to-look-at people.

Great climate, pretty faces, an exceptional standard of living—small wonder the island kingdom frequently topped the list of happiest places in the world to live, and small wonder that few spoke out against the status quo of the monarchy.

Beside her, Dante was now on the phone as they left the city limits and went onto the flat plain that, though interspersed by villages and hamlets, was mostly agricultural, consisting of vineyards that produced the unique grape species that made the wine produced here famous the world over.

She didn't know if the tension she could feel in him was connected to the conversation he was having, or his recent declaration of intent. Given her tendency to hear what she wanted, she tried to retain a sense of proportion.

There was nothing proportionate about the palace that loomed into view. It was visible for miles around because of its position on a hill that rose in the middle of a flat plain. She felt *heavier* as she looked at it—not physically, more emotionally. This might be some people's happiest place to live, but it had not been hers!

A perfect defensive position, the history books she had pored over had explained, before they spoke of the family who had taken control of the island five hundred years earlier, and the generations' contributions to the towering edifice to their wealth and power.

The palace was not a home, or even a fortress, which it originally had been; it was a statement of power and in reality a small city covering many acres of ground. The main body was devoted to state apartments, but many wings and towers were private apartments housing family. Other areas, like the world-famous art gallery, were a draw for international tourists and open to the public at certain times of the year.

The closer they got, the more daunting it became.

'That's a big sigh.'

Her head turned from the window. If the expression in the blue depths was an accurate reflection of the thoughts she had been so deeply lost in, they were not happy ones. In the time it took him to push away the inconvenient slug of guilt, the shadow vanished. Beatrice really had got good at hiding her feelings…which was a good thing, he acknowledged, but also…*sad*.

His lips tightened at the intrusion of emotion, and he wondered if there was such a thing as sympathy pregnancy hormones. He'd heard of sympathy about labour pains.

'You were wishing you were somewhere else?'

The question was as much to silence the mocking voice as anything else, but it opened the door to a question he had exerted a lot of effort to avoid. *With someone else?*

He had not forgotten her explosive reaction when he had casually dropped the subject into the conversation. His *innocent* comment had produced such an explosive response that you had to wonder if her overreaction was not about guilt.

Why guilt? asked the voice in his head. *Just because you have chosen to be celibate doesn't mean she has to follow suit...*

The golden skin stretched over the slashing angle of his cheekbones tightened, emphasising his dramatically perfect facial contours as he fought a brief internal battle to delete the images that came with the acknowledgement.

Celibacy was not a natural state, at least it wasn't for him. Sex, just plain, uncomplicated, emotion-free sex of the variety he used to enjoy, was a great stress-buster.

So, problem solved, mocked the voice in

his head, *except you don't want sex, you want sex with Beatrice.*

'Wishing…?' she echoed, breaking into his thoughts.

Wishing was not going to be much practical help at this moment. Her time was better spent mentally preparing herself for what lay ahead.

As their eyes connected Beatrice pushed out a laugh that held no amusement, while Dante told himself that she would not have future relationships; he would be enough for her.

He would enjoy being enough for her.

'Wishing is for little girls who want to marry a prince. I was never one of those little girls.' One of life's little, or in this case massive, ironies. 'Actually, I was still thinking about Carl. I wanted you to know that I think he is very brave.'

She had liked Carl on the occasions they had met. He had been about the only member of the Velazquez family other than Reynard who had made her feel welcome.

'So do I.'

'We wouldn't be here today if it wasn't for Carl's choices. I wonder sometimes where we would be, don't you?'

Dante leaned back, his head against the

corner of the sumptuously upholstered limo interior as he turned his body towards her, his languid pose at odds with the tension in his jaw and the watchful stillness in his face.

Embarrassed now and wishing she'd never started this rather one-sided conversation, she dodged his stare.

'Say whatever it is you need to say. If you're going to explode there is no one here to hear.'

There was a hint of defiance in her face as she responded. 'Doesn't it ever occur to you that when we got married we never planned, we never spoke about where we would live or anything?'

He dismissed her comment with a flick of his long brown fingers, irritation at her persistence sliding into his eyes. 'I have homes.'

'Across the world, I know—the penthouse in New York, the LA beachfront villa, the Paris apartment. Yes, you own endless properties, but not *homes*.'

'I am sure you are going to tell me why my real-estate portfolio seems to bother you so much.'

'Did you plan for your life to change at all? Was I ever meant to be more than a pretty accessory?'

'Well, my life has changed now.'

'Because of Carl, and the baby,' she conceded, dashing a hand across her face. 'But not out of choice, not because you got married. People who commit plan a future. We never did. That's all I was trying to say.'

'You were never pretty. You were, you are, beautiful.'

His voice, low and driven, sent a siren shudder down her spine, and as her eyes connected with the heat in his whatever she had been about to say vanished from her head, leaving nothing but a whisper of smoke.

She squeezed her eyes closed, pushed both hands into her hair as she shook her head to shake free the sensual fog and gave vent to a low groan of frustration, before fixing him with a baleful glare that gradually faded to one suggestive of tired defeat.

'Please do not change the subject.'

'I was—'

'You haven't got a clue what I'm talking about, have you?' she said wearily.

'We—'

'No, there was never a *we*.' She forced a smile, struggling to inject some lightness into this conversation, which she wished she had never started. 'I was always a bad fit, not just here. I never would have fitted into your playboy lifestyle. I was always pretending to be something I'm not.'

'In my bed?'

She coloured. 'No, not there,' she admitted, her eyes sliding from the suggestive heat in his.

'Why do I get the feeling that all this is leading up to a declaration of hostilities?'

'Not hostilities, just a declaration of intent.'

'You are warning me.' He sounded astonished at the concept.

'I'm telling you that I'm not fitting in any more. I'm being me. I owe myself, and this baby, that much. I never want him to look at me and feel ashamed that—' She stopped, realising a heartbeat after him where she had been going.

'You're still very angry with your mother, aren't you?'

'No…no…' she stammered out, disturbed by his perception. 'Not angry, I just… I don't want to be her.'

'You are not her and, for the record, I have no problem with you being yourself.'

She stopped and followed the direction of Dante's gaze through the tinted window. His eyes flickered to the edifice that dominated the landscape.

'Home, for me these days be it ever so humble.' He glanced her way. 'For us?'

She didn't react to the question, just nodded. 'It is beautiful. I always thought that it looked like something from a dream.'

Up close it looked real and solid, but it was not the carved stone that made her stomach tighten with nerves, it was the life inside it. A life she had never fitted into.

She had not married Dante because of his royal connections, but *despite* them. An inner voice of caution had told her she was playing out of her league, but she'd been too intoxicated by loving this incredible man and the baby they had created together to listen, and anyway he had never traded on his royalty. Dante didn't need to.

It was not his title, his blue blood or his wealth that made people listen when he spoke. She could hardly deny there was a sexual element to it; his sheer physical presence made an impact, but it was more he had an aura, a natural charisma—he was the sort of man who dominated any space he occupied.

She had turned away from him again but was no less conscious of his presence as she trained her eyes on the massive gates across the arched entrance that slid open as they approached. In profile, the purity of her golden features was quite breath-catching.

'Dream or nightmare?' he murmured sardonically.

She smiled faintly, but didn't turn her head, so he allowed himself the indulgence of allowing his gaze to drift in a slow lingering sweep over her smooth, glowing skin. The resulting tightening in his guts was as painful as it was inevitable.

She turned her head and caught a look on his face that was almost pain. 'Don't worry. I will try to make this work.'

'I never doubted it.'

CHAPTER NINE

'So, what is the cover story?'

'Cover story?'

'I mean, what is the press office going to release, or are you keeping me undercover for the time being?'

'I have a cupboard you would fit right in.'

His wilful imagination conjured a scenario where she was not alone in that space, their bodies pressed against—

He sucked in sense-sustaining air through flared nostrils and tried to halt the heat building inside him before it reached the critical point of no return.

His flippancy caused her frown to deepen. 'You know what I mean. I am assuming you want me to keep a low profile.'

'The press office will not be briefing.'

She stared. 'But that's—'

'The way it is. If asked directly the response will be the family is happy to have you back.'

'Irony, that's a change.'

'*I* am happy to have you back.'

'Oh!' She faintly willed herself not to read too much into his words, or the expression in his eyes.

'Is anyone going to believe that?'

It was clear to him that she didn't, and Dante realised that her belief was all that mattered to him. He wanted to be the father of their child; he wanted to be half the man she deserved.

'I thought you weren't a fan of the spin doctors. Would you prefer to be in their hands or mine?'

She stared at the long brown tapering fingers extended for her scrutiny and felt her stomach muscles dissolve as she remembered how they felt on her skin, stroking...touching...

'Spin...you mean I don't like being patronised, manipulated and talked over? Yes, I am a bit odd that way.'

'Welcome to my world.'

The world she had been glad to leave. 'Nobody would dare patronise you—and as for talk over you!' She gave a hoot of laughter.

'Present company excepted?'

She fought off a smile in response to the gleam in his eyes, a gleam that held enough warmth to make her oversensitive stomach flip dangerously.

'I hate them, but they were right, weren't they?'

Despite her misgivings the supercilious suits had been right: nothing had leaked about the divorce proceedings. Certainly not to the journalists and opportunistic paparazzi who had dogged her steps for the first few weeks, along with the security detail that she had decided not to confront Dante about. They were discreet, which was a plus—there were days that she'd forgotten they were there.

The press pack had gradually lost interest when she hadn't been seen doing anything even vaguely newsworthy; she never reacted to questions and had no social media presence. A nun had a more interesting life, someone had written, and there were only so many times they could report on the length of her legs.

Beatrice had concluded being boring had its plus points.

'Did they fly back with us?'

He shook his head. 'They?'

'Seb, Roberto, Luis and the one with the really nicely trimmed beard. The security detail—my minders.' Did he really think she wouldn't notice just because she hadn't kicked up a fuss?

'You knew their names.' He swore under his breath—so much for covert surveillance. 'They stayed behind. Your sister could be a press target. You are safe with me.'

Strangely, considering how objectionable she had initially found their presence, she felt oddly comforted by this information, and felt quite guilty about the fact.

'*Safe?*' She slung him an ironic look and, rubbing the bridge of her nose, pushed back in her seat, digging her head into the soft leather upholstery to ease the muscles of her aching neck before she turned her head in his direction.

'You *really* think it will be that easy? I just reappear and it's all happy families? Your family must be planning your next marriage. Won't me being here throw a spanner in the works?'

'Oh, I think they were doing that before you left.'

She had been joking but, looking at his face, she wasn't sure he was. Of course it made sense. He was going to be King one day and he needed a queen and why wait? It was all about continuity.

Ignoring the sharp stab of something that could be jealousy, or loss, or hurt, she managed a flippant comeback to prove to herself as much as him that her heart was not broken.

'So, any prospective candidates standing out yet?'

'Perhaps you're better placed than most to decide what would make my perfect bride.'

'Are you flirting with me?'

Before she could react to his wicked grin, she realised that while they had been speaking they had entered the palace proper. The cars in front of them and behind had peeled away at some point, and they were now drawing up between the two elaborate stone fountains that stood outside the porticoed entrance to the private apartments she had left eight months ago.

She sat there, fighting a deep reluctance to get out of the car. Once she did it would all seem real, which up to that point it hadn't. She felt as if stepping onto the gravel would be akin to ripping a scab off a healing wound, releasing the pleasure and pain of past memories.

She took a deep breath and reminded herself this was the new, improved Beatrice. Sane Beatrice who did not lose her mind, or become malleable mush when breathing the same air as Dante.

'I am a bit tired after the journey,' she said, setting the scene for when she excused herself. A bit of aloneness was looking very tempting right now.

'*Ah...*'

She looked at him, bristling with suspicion. 'Do you mind translating that *"Ah"* into something I won't like?'

'There is a reception tonight for the French ambassador and his wife. It was arranged some time ago and it was deemed to be diplomatically unwise to cancel. We have already postponed once. Mother had a headache—actually she was hung-over.'

'Fine, don't worry, I can amuse myself.'

'Ah...'

She regarded him with narrowed eyes.

'The point is that should the ambassador become aware that you are here your non-attendance could be construed as an insult.'

'You even sound like a diplomat.'

'A bit harsh, Bea.'

She fought off a grin. 'Couldn't you say I had a headache or something?' She wasn't at all sure she didn't, she decided, rubbing her temples with her fingertips before she gave a resigned sigh. 'All right, tell me the worst.'

His expression tensed. 'There is no question of you attending if you feel unwell. I will have the physician visit. In fact, this might be a good idea. You've had a long day and you shouldn't overexert yourself. Stress isn't good for the baby.'

'I'm fine,' she promised, adopting a businesslike tone. 'So, who will be at this dinner?'

As he listed the guests she gave several eye-rolls, interspersed with theatrical sighs.

'So basically, the snootiest, stuffiest—'

'I'm sure you'll cope admirably,' he cut back with an utter lack of sympathy that made her eyes narrow. 'Just be yourself.'

She opened her mouth and closed it, realising that this was almost like talking to the man she had fallen in love with, the one who didn't give a damn about protocol. They had always shared the same sense of humour, and appreciation of irony.

'Oh, I'll be fine after a bottle of champagne,' she said airily and watched the look of utter horror cross his face before adding with a sigh, *Joke...?* You remember those?' Nine months of sobriety was not going to be a big ask for her—her normal alcohol consumption mostly involved nursing a glass for the sake of being sociable.

Not that she was making a statement. She had just never really liked the taste.

'I remember *everything*, Beatrice.'

The silence stretched as *something* in the atmosphere of the enclosed space changed. Impossible to put a name to, mainly because she didn't dare to, but it made her pulse race and her throat dry as he leaned in.

When he broke the silence all she was thinking about was his mouth and the way he tasted, the way he always tasted.

'Let's skip the dinner and go to bed!'

The feelings fizzing up inside her were making her breathless. 'You're not serious.'

He arched a brow and gave a wicked grin. 'I don't know, am I…?'

His laughter followed her out of the car as she hurried to put some safe distance between them.

She marched towards the door and past the men who stood either side, staring straight ahead. They wore bright gold-trimmed ceremonial uniforms, but the guns slung over their shoulders were not ceremonial but unfortunately very real.

It wasn't until she entered the echoing hallway with its row of glittering chandeliers suspended from a high vaulted carved ceiling that Beatrice took a deep breath, fighting against the tangle of jumbled memories that crowded her head.

For a split second panic almost took control. She had no idea if she was standing, sitting or lying, then, as she exhaled and the panicked thud in her ears of her own heartbeat receded, she was able to reel herself back to something approaching control.

The breath left her parted lips in a slow, measured, calming hiss before she turned, masking her emotions under a slightly shaky smile.

Dante was standing a couple of feet away, his hands shoved in the pockets of his well-cut trousers. He had been watching her almost lose it. The enormity of what he was asking her to do hit him between the eyes like the proverbial blunt object.

She was distracted from this uncomfortable possibility by the fact that he was standing right in front of a larger-than-life portrait of a previous King of San Macizo, though this painting captured him when he had been Crown Prince.

She had noticed the striking similarity between the two men the first time she'd walked in, though she'd not then noted the far more modest portraits of his several wives hidden on a wall in a rarely used part of the building.

Legend had it that the first, rather plain-looking wife, who had died in childbirth, had been his one true love, but then legends rarely had substance. Still, it was a pleasingly romantic tale and she had liked to think it true.

The illusion that the figure staring down with hauteur etched on his carved features had actually stepped out of the frame lasted several blinks.

The man standing watching her had all the hauteur along with the perfect symmetry of features his ancestor had possessed. Had his ancestor possessed the same earthy sensual quality that Dante had? If he had, the artist hadn't captured it, though with those lips you had to wonder.

She pulled her shoulders back, feeling some sympathy for the long-ago wives, wondering if they too had stopped trying to figure out why their responses to their prince bypassed logic or common sense. Like her, had they just come to accept and guard against it as much as possible?

Dante watched as she made a visible effort to gather herself, but the expression on her face reminded him of a fighter who had taken too many punches, and maybe she had in the emotional sense.

He was prepared for the guilt and he accepted it. He had anticipated it. What he had not anticipated was that seeing her here, in this setting, would actually make him *more* aware of the ache that he had lived with since her departure. An ache he had refused to acknowledge, an ache that indicated weakness he couldn't own up to.

His upbringing had developed a strong streak of self-sufficiency in Dante. He had been sent to boarding school at six, where the policy was to discourage contact between siblings, the theory being part of the institute's ethos that was intended to develop a strength of character and independence.

Which in Dante's experience in practical terms translated as an ability to look after number one ahead of all others, and he had learnt the lesson. Well, the option had been enduring the misery of those who didn't, and there had been more than a few who'd never understood that showing weakness exposed you to the bullies.

Dante never had shown weakness; he had gone into the school system privileged and come out privileged and selfish as hell. The strategies developed at a tender age were coping mechanisms that had stood him in good stead. One kicked in now, stopping him acknowledging the emptiness.

'I can make your excuses?'

Her chin went up. 'I can make my own,' she began hotly and stopped, an expression of guilt spreading across her face as she saw through his offhand manner. 'There is no need to be worried about the baby. I would never do anything that put him at risk.'

'Him?'

'Or her.'

'Do you want to know?'

'I'm not sure...' Sadness settled across her features. Their first pregnancy had not lasted long enough for it to be a question she had been asked. 'Will the sex matter?' she asked, pushing the sadness away. She knew it would never go away, and she knew it was all right to feel it, but she didn't want it to overshadow the miracle that was happening to her body now.

'Matter?'

'I mean, can a female succeed to the throne?'

Her eyes widened with shock as she saw his hand move towards her; she gave a little gasp as he placed his hand on her flat belly.

'By the time it matters to this one's future, she will.'

His hand fell away, and she wanted to put it back. A dangerous shiver ran through her body as warning bells clanged in her ears.

'You intend to change things.'

'Baby steps.'

This time the words did not injure; they made her smile.

The lines around his eyes crinkled, totally disarming her fragile defences, which were jolted back into life when he angled his head towards the curving staircase with the elaborate wrought-iron balustrade that led to their private apartments that stretched along the first floor of this wing.

'I actually think tonight is a good idea. I'm going to see your parents at some point. It might as well be now.' Meeting them in company would hopefully limit their ability to make snide digs. After all, appearances were everything in this household. 'What time…?'

'An hour?'

Dante stopped with his back to the glass-fronted lift and nodded towards the staircase. He knew that Beatrice was not keen on enclosed spaces and would walk up a heart-stopping number of steps to avoid a lift. 'After you, you know the way.'

'Which room?' she began and stopped, her eyes flying wide as his meaning hit home. 'I'm in our...*your* room?' she blurted. It was only seconds before a flush began to work its way up her neck.

Their room, but he would have long vacated it.

He was probably trying one of those suitable candidates for size in another room?

The images that accompanied the possibilities made her feel nauseous and then mad because she had been suffering and celibate and it only seemed fair that he should have been too. But then life here had never been fair or balanced; it worried her that she needed to remind herself.

'I never got around to moving my things out.'

The warning made her freeze. 'You mean you're still...!' She would have laughed outright at the suggestion that he would have been personally involved in any moving if his comment hadn't raised a number of issues. Mainly, was he assuming that they would be sharing the room? She could see how spending the night with him in the ski chalet might have led to this assumption.

'Your things are still there.'

The casual throwaway information added

another layer of confusion. It could've been a housekeeping error, except such a thing did not exist inside the palace walls.

There was literally an army of people that would have made it possible for her to wake up in the morning and not have to do a single thing for herself right up to the end of the day.

There was always someone hovering, ready to relieve you of the burden of tying your own shoelace should you find that a bore, or too tiresome. It had been one of the *royal* things that she'd never got the hang of. She simply couldn't ask someone to perform a task that she was more than capable of completing herself, and she couldn't for the life of her see how it was demeaning to be seen making her own sandwich or washing out her own tights, but both had been activities that had been frowned on.

She had expected Dante to laugh with her at the sheer absurdity of people having so much time on their hands that they thought sandwich-making was a sin worth passing up the chain of command when she told him about her sugar-coated reprimand—the sugar had made it so much *less*, not *more*, acceptable—but he had just looked at her with a frown indenting his forehead.

'Can't you just go with the flow for once? Is it really worth the argument?'

It was the moment she had realised that they had stopped laughing at the same things. Actually Dante had stopped laughing altogether—that Dante had gone forever. Sometimes she wondered if he had ever really existed.

There was sadness and regret in the shaded look she angled up at his lean face.

'It's your room. I'll take one of the others.'

'It was our room,' he said without emphasis. 'You might as well take it. I think you'll find most of your things where you left them.' Nobody had questioned his instructions to touch nothing, not even him, though now he might have to face the question that he had avoided because Beatrice was going to.

He'd kept telling himself that he'd get around to it, that he didn't like the idea of someone else touching Beatrice's things, but somehow it was a task he'd kept putting off.

He didn't sleep there any more; he slept, the little he did, on a couch in his office. Not because he was avoiding anything. It was a matter of convenience.

There was always a spare set of clothes in his office, and his running gear. He could shower there, he could shrug on a fresh shirt. It worked because he didn't keep office hours.

He wasn't avoiding anything. It wasn't in any way symbolic; it wasn't as if he were in denial. Bea had gone and it was better for her and better for him.

She was looking at him with a puzzled expression.

'But I wasn't coming back.' She had assumed her belongings would have been boxed as soon as she had gone. She had wondered more than once about asking for them to be sent on.

He shrugged, appearing exasperated by her persistence as he dragged a hand through his dark hair and sighed, managing by the flicker of an eyebrow to make her feel she was making a big deal out of nothing at all.

Maybe because you *want* it to be a big deal for him? Maybe you want it to hurt for him too? Before the horror of acknowledgement hit home, she pushed away the preposterous idea, conscious that she was guilty of over-analysing.

'But you are back.'

She couldn't argue with that, but it meant sleeping in the same bed they had shared... as if this weren't hard enough anyway. She'd stepped out of this life—stepping back in was going to present challenges regardless of where she slept.

This time, when his hand curved around her cheek, she did let her cheek fall into it.

'Look, I know this is hard for you but—' He broke off, cursing as the opening of a door to their left made Beatrice jump away from him.

Giggles entered the hallway a moment before two uniformed figures. One saw Dante and stopped so quickly that the smaller figure bumped into her.

'*Scusi*, Highness...' Eyes round with shock, her face pink with embarrassment, she dropped a curtsy and the woman behind her followed suit.

Dante addressed them, speaking Italian, and they responded in the same language. Considering she had been boastful about her language ability earlier, Beatrice didn't have a clue what was being said. Her brain wasn't functioning through the jam of conflicting emotions in her head.

She stood there with a fixed smile throughout the exchange and one thing was clear: if her arrival had not been officially announced, it had now.

He gave a sardonic smile as the women

vanished through the door they had entered and closed it behind them.

'They think I don't know they use this suite as a shortcut when we're away,' he said, sounding amused. 'Don't worry, word will get around we are back.'

'My ears are already burning.'

'They'd be burning some more if we slept at opposite ends of the building,' he predicted drily.

'Was that ever an option?' she asked, with a catch in her voice.

He held her eyes and her insides tightened as he didn't say a word. The look, even without the shake of his head, was enough.

'But relax,' he added as she swung away from him. 'There's still the bed in my dressing room if that is what you want.'

Walking behind her, he watched as she almost missed the next step but after a pause carried on walking.

He caught up with her, pulling level as he added in a low voice that dragged like rough velvet across her nerve endings, *'Remember?'*

Her hand tightened on the banister as she stopped and flung him an anguished look. 'Why are you doing this, Dante?'

Remember? Of course she remembered... She'd made her complaint after Dante had not slipped into their bed before three in the morning and had then been up before six for two weeks straight. It had been intended to ignite a discussion about his unhealthy work-life balance.

That had always been optimistic. Dante took the entire caveman-of-few-words thing to extremes, missing the point entirely and, working under the assumption she was concerned about her own disturbed beauty sleep, he'd had a bed put up in the adjoining dressing room so that he would not disturb her.

The one occasion he had used it she had lasted five minutes before she had left the massive bed they'd shared and joined him, sliding in beside him in the narrow bed. Images floated into her head, warm bodies entwined, his need to lose himself in her, her need to give. The cumulative effect had always generated heat.

She felt heat now ripple through her body and, resisting the temptation to feed it, lowered her eyes, her glance snagging on his strong brown fingers that were curled lightly around the cool metal of the banister a bare inch away from her own.

Conscious of the tingling and the tug, she pulled her own hand away and pressed it against her stomach.

'I really don't think our sleeping arrangements are anyone else's business,' she said, even though she knew this view would not be shared. The palace was filled with spies loyal to differing factions, the King's spies, the Queen's spies... Everyone took sides, at least that was how it had felt to her, or maybe she had been infected by the paranoia of the claustrophobic life inside the palace walls?

Her eyes went to Dante's face. Presumably he now had his own army of spies reporting to him. 'And now you're *making* the rules.'

She hitched her bag onto her shoulder, not anticipating that her remark would evoke much reaction, certainly not the ripple of complex emotions she saw flicker across his face.

Had she inadvertently hit a nerve?

'Well, don't you?'

'So is that how you think of me? A dictator?' He vented a wry laugh as they began to climb the sweep of stairs together. 'I sometimes think it would make life easier.'

He felt he was not just combating his own perceived inexperience but a father who, while he was reluctant to relinquish any power, was equally reluctant to leave the golf course for a long boring meeting, and senior courtiers who, accustomed to winding their

King round their collective fingers, thought modernity a dirty word and equated stability with immobility.

She realised they were standing outside the open door to Dante's study. Opposite was a small salon, where her Italian tutor used to try and be polite about her progress. They were a few doors down from the bedroom suite they had shared, but he went directly to the first door and opened it.

'This is me. I've had the doors to both the adjoining suites opened up, so if you hear any noise you'll know…'

Beatrice immediately felt foolish for making such an unnecessary issue out of the room situation. 'Not very likely, the walls are about ten feet thick.'

'And there are locks on all the interconnecting doors, should you be concerned I might ravish you.'

'Maybe I'm worried that I might ravish you. It wouldn't be the first time,' she flung back recklessly.

He stood there, his eyes burning into her… Very slowly he raised his hand and, with one finger, tilted her face up to him.

'What are *you* trying to do, Beatrice?' he said, turning her own words back on her.

His hand dropped and she gave a shuddering sigh of shame, tears standing out in her eyes as she passed a shaky hand across her mouth.

'I'm sorry,' she whispered, before turning and running down the corridor to her own bedroom door. She felt his eyes burning into her back but she didn't turn around, she didn't breathe, until she was safe behind the closed door.

CHAPTER TEN

SHE STOOD THERE, back against the door, her
eyes squeezed tight shut until she heard the
faint sound of a door closing.

Up to this point the necessity of maintaining rigid defences had kept the exhaustion
of the day, as much emotional as physical, at
bay. Now as her shoulders slumped a wave
of deep weariness swept over her.

Struggling against the memories being in
this room evoked, images that were buzzing
in her head like a swarm of wasps, she headed
for the bed and sank down.

She felt her eyes fill but she was too tired
for tears. How had she allowed herself to get
into this position?

By saying yes to Dante—so no change
there!

She was here and this was not the time for
a post-mortem as to how she had put herself

in this position. She just had to deal and get on with it.

This was about the baby. A soft smile curved her lips as she rested her hand on the non-existent swell of her belly.

'Your daddy loves you,' she whispered, hoping that it were true.

Dashing the hint of moisture that had seeped from the corners of her eyes, she gave a loud sniff. Puffy eyes were not a good look for a formal dinner. She pulled herself up off the bed and stood there, ignoring the heaviness in her legs and the ache in her chest. She didn't examine her immediate surroundings; instead she opened the wide interconnecting doors into the adjoining room. Outside the bedroom she was able to breathe a little easier.

Wandering through the rooms where she had lived, it was all the same, but not really.

It took her a few moments to realise that though the antique furniture was still the same, some of the heavier items that she had requested to be stowed away, like the priceless, but to her mind ugly, set of cabriole-legged chairs, had been returned. The walls were covered in the paintings that had been in situ when she had arrived; the ones that were more to her taste had presumably been put back in some vault labelled not cultured enough.

As she wandered from room to room it dawned on her that actually *all* the personal touches she had introduced had vanished from these rooms.

She had been wiped from the rooms and probably Velazquez family history.

In the west-facing sitting room where she liked to spend her morning, the light was so beautiful, she glanced wistfully at the carved stone mantle where the natural sculpted driftwood she had collected during walks on the beach was no longer evident. In its place there were pieces of delicate porcelain, which were beautiful but had none of the tactile quality she had loved.

Likewise, the church candles she had lit in the evening when it was too warm for a fire no longer filled the elaborate grate and the vases she had filled with bare branches now held rigid formal floral displays.

Without the bright splashes of colour from the cushions and throws she had scattered throughout, the rooms looked very different from how they had in her mind. Even the bookshelves had become colour-coordinated and stripped of her piles of paperbacks. There was not a single thing that could have been termed eclectic in any part of the apartment.

Leaving the places where her presence had been clinically expunged, she reopened the door to the bedroom and, with a deep sustaining breath, walked inside.

It was just a room.

No, she realised, it was the *same* room.

The same room she had walked out of eight months earlier. After the complete removal of anything that was remotely her in the other rooms, the contrast was dramatic. The room was like some sort of time capsule where her presence had been preserved.

It really was almost as though she had just walked out of the room. Stunned, she stood poised in the doorway, her wide blue eyes transmitting shock before she stepped inside.

She ran her fingers across the paperback on the bedside table, the spine still stretched open at the page she had been reading, before walking over to the dressing table where the messy pile of earrings, bracelets and makeup she had left behind still seemed to be in exactly the same place she had left them.

Every item she touched carried distracting memories, which she struggled to push away. Instead, aiming for a practical focus, she pressed the hidden button and the massive walk-in wardrobe slid silently open while the overhead recessed lights burst into life, along with those over the mirrored wall ahead, reflecting her image back at her.

She blinked, and saw her sister's face appear, her dark eyes laughing as she walked inside the wardrobe she declared to be bigger than the entire flat they had once shared. She was laughing as she spun gracefully around, her arms spread wide as she took in the space.

The image was so real that Beatrice found the corners of her mouth lifting as she remembered Maya's reaction, then wobbling as the memory of her sister's assessment swam to the surface of the recollections.

'Oh, my God. Perfect for people who love looking at themselves.' Her husky laughter had rung out as she'd stepped inside and begun to open myriad doors to reveal racks and shelves; her laughter had turned to silent awe.

'When you said you'd stopped off in Paris to shop…' She'd rubbed her fingers across a silk catsuit that they had both last seen and admired in a high-end magazine spread. 'When will you ever wear all this?'

Beatrice had shrugged. 'I know. It's crazy.' How was she to have known that the personal shopper thought her trying something on and saying she liked it equated to *I'll take it—in several colours*?

Dante had laughed at her horror and overruled her when she'd announced her intention to send back the stacks of clothes that had come draped over hangers inside cellophane wrappers and in layers of tissue paper in ribbon-tied boxes.

'You want me to charter a plane for your clothes? Imagine the carbon footprint,' he had taunted.

Beatrice pushed away the lingering memory and replaced his voice in her head with an amused Maya saying that she might work her way through this lot in ten years or so, if she changed outfit three times a day and four on a weekend.

She never had because she hadn't stayed for ten years; she had barely stuck it out for ten months, and now she was back and all the suppressed emotions had surfaced, combining with her baby hormones to make her feel raw and vulnerable.

She dashed a hand across her eyes; she was just too tired of soul-searching. Today had gone as well as she could have expected.

Dante seemed to be making a genuine effort for the baby's sake, and that was the problem.

It was for the baby. She wanted him to want her, to need her as much as she needed him.

Giving her head a tiny brisk shake, she pushed away the thoughts and turned to a section that was devoted to evening wear.

After pulling out a few dresses she finally settled on a full-length white silk gown, the style a modern take on classic Grecian. The heavy fabric swirled on the hanger as she held it up. It left one shoulder bare, the hand-embroidered sections on the skirt alleviating the stark purity of the design.

It took her half an hour from choosing suitable shoes to complement her choice—the plain court style was secondary to the fact they were made of a silver jewelled glittering fabric and the spiky heels elongated her long legs even more—to putting the finishing touches to her hair. The fact the ends were still damp made it easier to pin it into a simple topknot and at the last minute she pulled out some loose shiny strands and let the shiny wisps fall, creating a softening effect against her cheeks and long neck.

She added a light spritz of her favourite perfume, ignoring the voice in her head that said it had only become her favourite since Dante had said it was his, when there was a tap on the door that connected the adjoining suite.

She had time to suck in a hurried restorative breath, take in the flush on her cheeks and the sparkle that was part excitement, part fear in her wide-spaced eyes, before the door opened and Dante stepped into the room, his dark head slightly bent as he adjusted the cufflinks at his right wrist.

It gave Beatrice time to close her mouth and paste in place an expression that fell disastrously short of neutral, but at least she wasn't licking her lips or drooling too obviously.

A lot of men looked good in formal evening wear, the tailoring could hide a multitude of sins, but Dante had nothing to hide and the perfect tailoring emphasised the breadth of his shoulders, the length of his legs and...well, his perfect *everything*. One day she might be able to view his earthly male beauty with objectivity, but that day was a long way off.

She felt the heat unfurl low in her belly and ignored it as she opened her mouth to offer to straighten his tie and changed her mind. Less wisdom and more self-preservation as she remembered more than one occasion when a tie-straightening offer had made them late for an official engagement.

Dante took his time over the cuff adjustment to give the heat in his blood time to cool and recover from the razor-sharp spasm of mind-numbing desire that had spiked through him in that brief moment before he'd lowered his gaze, the electricity thrumming in a steady stream through his body.

She always had been the chink in his armour, the beautiful downfall for a man who, over the years, had become smugly confident in his ability to control his carnal appetites, not have them control him.

And once again she was carrying his child. He had never expected that they would be here again, but the knowledge she was carrying his child only increased the carnal attraction.

He performed another necessary adjustment and lifted his head. He had regained some level of control, but there were limits. He didn't even attempt to prevent his eyes drifting up from her feet to the top of her shining head, knowing the effort would be useless. He recognised it was a dangerous indulgence, but things could be contained so long as he didn't touch her. Experience had taught him that the explosion would be madness.

Everywhere his eyes touched shivers zig-zagged over the surface of her skin, awakening nerve pathways, making her ache. The smoky heat in his stare and the clenched tension in his jaw were some sop to her frustration. At least she wasn't the only one suffering.

'I'm ready,' she said, her voice brighter than the occasion justified. She could hear the tinge of desperation, she just hoped he couldn't.

The intensity of his hungry stare did not diminish and the longer it lasted, the harder it was for her to resist the impulse to fling herself at him. Then when he did break the silence his voice sounded so cool that she was relieved she had not reacted to it when it was quite possible that the heat she had felt pounding the air between them had been a product of her febrile imagination.

'So I see, punctual as always and, I imagine, just as impatient about being kept waiting, so you see… I didn't.' He extended a crooked arm and after a moment she moved forward to rest her hand lightly on it, aware as she did of the muscled strength of his forearm.

'You look perfect,' he said, without looking at her.

'Thank you.'

As they approached the shallow steps that led from the private apartment into the corridor that linked to what she thought of as the palace proper, Beatrice raised her gown slightly with her free hand, exposing her sparkling shoes.

The glitter caught Dante's attention; he arched a brow. 'What all the princesses are wearing these days?' he teased, not looking at her ankles any longer. His gaze had progressed to the long, lovely lines of her thighs outlined against the heavy silk fabric of her dress.

Though her heart was trying to climb its way out of her chest, she tried to replicate the blank look on the impassive faces of the two uniformed figures they were walking past.

'Do I look different?' She flashed him a worried look. She *felt* different. 'Do you think anyone will guess?'

He paused and, capturing her wrists, pulled her towards him. 'Would it matter if they did?'

'I know you think I'm being stupid about this.'

'It's your call.'

'Well, if anyone did guess,' she added on a philosophical note, 'it couldn't be any more excruciatingly awful than the last time the subject of babies came up at the dinner table.'

His blank expression made it obvious that he didn't have a clue what she was talking about.

Beatrice envied his amnesia. She would never, *could* never, forget the silence around the table that night, when she had responded to a thinly veiled hint when she had refused a glass of wine.

Suddenly everyone had been exchanging knowing glances and saying how very well she looked...positively glowing.

There had been any number of similar moments after the early loss of that first pregnancy where it had been made clear that should she prove to have good childbearing hips all her other shortcomings might be overlooked.

Dante didn't seem to realise how agonisingly embarrassing she'd found the entire situation. Previous to that night she had risen above the comments, had damped down her hurt over their insensitivity, but on that occasion something inside her had snapped. She had tried to do it Dante's way, it had been time for hers, and she had always found that the best way to deal with most situations was by being upfront, despite the fact that she'd agreed with Dante up to a point. It hadn't been anybody's business, but then no one had been staring at *his* belly waiting to see a royal bump!

Of course, there had never been any official acknowledgement of her miscarriage, but she'd known that her personal loss was the subject of palace gossip and speculation.

She had tried not to care, to rise above it, but as she'd looked around the table she'd known full well that there wasn't a single person present who didn't know the details, a single person who hadn't discussed her fertility.

Despite her outward composure her voice had shaken a little with the effort to control the surge of emotion inside as, looking at the woman seated opposite her, she'd deliberately pitched her words to reach the entire table as she'd remarked how much she loved children and hoped to have several.

The approving smiles that had followed this group-share announcement had faded when she'd gone on to explain that she would be following her own parents' example, that she wanted to adopt as well as give birth, but that she didn't plan on doing either just yet.

By the time she'd finished speaking the entire table had been sitting in shocked silence, broken finally by the King himself, who had announced quite simply that adoption for a member of the royal family was not an option, before proceeding to make a lot of pronouncements about bloodlines and breeding that had made her blood boil before he'd risen and left the table, indicating that the discussion was over.

So Dante hadn't leapt to her defence. She'd been prepared to cut him some slack as there hadn't been much opportunity once his father had gone into regal-pronouncement mode.

She hadn't expected to have Dante intervene on her behalf, she could defend herself, and the first lesson on royal protocol that she had learnt was that you didn't contradict the King, although she had seen Dante calmly face down his father, with an emphasis on the calm, when it had come to something he'd thought important. Dante had always emerged the victor without raising his voice, no matter how loud his father had got—but this had never happened when there were people present outside the immediate family, as there had been that night.

But she had been quite glad of his silently supportive arm around her shoulders as they'd returned to their apartments. It wasn't until the door had closed that she'd realised that the arm hadn't been supportive, more restraining, and Dante had been quite royally *unhappy* with her.

In fact he'd blamed her for reacting the way she had and making a situation where none had existed.

And now there *was* a situation.

'Are you all right?' he asked her now, scanning her face.

'A bit light-headed, that's all.'

'This is not a good idea,' he said, dragging out one of the ornately carved chairs that were set at intervals along the wall.

'No,' Beatrice said, resisting his efforts to push her into it. 'I didn't get all dressed up for nothing. I really am fine. Please stop looking at me as though I'm an unexploded time bomb. The baby is fine. I am fine.'

'You are not fine—you escaped and now you're back. The doors have closed and locked and you're wondering what the hell you were thinking of.' He smiled at her shocked expression. 'You think I have never felt that way?'

'You?'

He tipped his dark head and gave a faint twisted smile. 'I sometimes feel as if the walls are closing in on me.' His dark eyes lifted to the ornately carved ceiling high above.

'What do you do?' she asked, fascinated by

the new insight. Did Dante ever think about escaping?

'I used to escape in your arms, inside you, *cara.*'

'Dante?' Her stomach clenched with helpless desire as their eyes met.

He stroked her cheek with one finger. 'Lately I remind myself that I am here to change things, that I can knock down walls, change mindsets. So long as no one guesses I don't have a clue what I'm doing I might become a man my son is not too ashamed of.'

She was moved beyond words and for several moments could not speak. 'You do know what you're doing,' she protested indignantly.

'Do I?' he said, self-mockery gleaming in his eyes. 'Frankly,' he continued in the manner of someone making a clean breast of it, 'it doesn't matter so long as people think you know what you're doing.'

She took an impetuous step towards him and almost stumbled. He caught her elbow to steady her, his own heart thudding hard in reaction to the burst of adrenalin in his bloodstream.

'Be careful!' The surge of protective concern edged his voice with gravel.

It was possibly good advice.

'Those heels are a little high, considering...'

Her smile of gratitude half formed froze
in place as the warmth in his eyes hardened.
'Considering *what*?'

'Isn't that obvious?' he said, seemingly
oblivious to the danger in her voice.

'Please do not try and wrap me up in cotton
wool, Dante. I am a woman, not an incubator,
and I'm pregnant, not ill.' Having made her
point, she hoped—it was hard to tell from his
expression—she didn't dwell on the subject.
She took a deep breath and moved the conversation on. 'So, who is there tonight, again?'

Him going over the guest list gave her the
opportunity to gather a little of her composure.

'Wow, it sounds like a fun evening.' Her
mocking smile faded as she looked up at him,
conscious of the gaping gap that had grown
between them as they'd walked. Was there
ever a time when she could have bridged it
without a baby?

If so, it had gone, because without the baby
she would not be here.

She damped the beads of moisture along
her upper lip as she struggled to banish the
questions and doubts swirling in her head.

'What am I even doing here?'

'Is that a rhetorical question?'

She shook her head. 'Sorry, just a mild

panic attack, but don't worry, I'll be on my best behaviour.'

'No, don't.'

Her blue eyes fluttered wide. 'What?'

'All I want is for you to be yourself.' Infuriating, foot-in-mouth but always honest self. 'I get tired...of people...'

'Polishing your ego?'

He gave a cynical grin. 'I'm sometimes tempted to announce the world is flat just to watch them admire my amazing intellect.'

She laughed. 'I'd pay good money to see that.'

'It isn't too late to change your mind.'

'Yes, it is,' she countered as they passed into the palace proper, as she called it in her head.

The carpet underfoot now was inches deep and scarlet with a border of gold; the crystal chandeliers glittering overhead lit the long corridor that seemed to stretch into infinity, guarded by rows of portraits of more of Dante's ancestors, ancestors' wives, children and dogs and, in one case, a leopard with a jewelled collar looking almost as supercilious as its mistress.

If the intention was to impress or intimidate, it did both.

They were the last to join the guests and

family in the drawing room, where the mingling involved a lot of diamond tiaras, med-
als on lapels and stiffly formal conversation.

'Did all conversations stop just now, or did
I forget to put my clothes on?' Beatrice asked,
her cheeks already starting to ache from the
effort of maintaining her meaningless smile.

Her comment invited Dante to see her
naked, every sleek, smooth, glorious inch
of her, and his imagination obliged, which
meant his smile was forced around the edges
and he felt the need to loosen his tie, an action which, across the room, earned a horri-
fied glare from his mother.

'Forget the gossips, we owe them no ex-
planations.'

She slung an 'easy for you to say' look
up at the tall, imposing figure of her husband as she gritted out through a clenched
smile, 'I feel like I've stumbled into one of
my nightmares. Do you think there are odds
on how long I'll stay this time?' She took a
deep breath and allowed her veiled blue gaze
to take in all the details. 'Wow, this really
is vintage Velazquez. Reminds me of everything I don't miss.'

'On the plus side, so is the champagne,'
Dante said, appropriating two flutes from a
passing waiter, then, realising what he'd done,

slammed them back down on the tray and selected the alternative sparkling water just before the Queen, wearing a staggering amount of diamonds, bore down on them.

'How delightful you look. Good flight?' The Queen greeted her with gracious frigidity and raised a pencilled eyebrow when Beatrice drained the glass of sparkling water in her hand.

The King appeared and ignored Beatrice, so she returned the favour.

'Dante, you are escorting the countess into dinner. You can't escort your wife.'

Dante smiled at his father. 'Actually, I can.' He held out his arm to Beatrice, who, after a pause, took it, and they went to join the other guests who were pairing off to process into the state banquet hall.

'If looks could kill.' She had enjoyed the expression on her father-in-law's face, but she enjoyed even more the feeling that she and Dante were on the same team.

'They don't.'

'Don't?'

'Kill. I have conducted pretty extensive research into the subject. There have been occasional reports of minor injuries but absolutely no fatalities.'

Beatrice's gurgle of laughter drew several

glances and several comments on what an attractive couple the future King and Queen made.

'Thanks for having my back.'

He looked down into her beautiful face and felt shame break loose inside him. She shouldn't be thanking him; it should have been something that she took for granted... but why would she? He had never had her back when it had counted.

He watched as she took a deep breath and straightened her shoulders, and felt the shame mingled now with pride. When had he ever acknowledged the courage she had shown?

She had wanted to blend in but she never would, he realised with a rush of pride, because she was better than them. Better than him, he decided, not immediately identifying the tightening in his chest as protective tenderness.

He didn't want her to blend in!

'I'm here if you need me.'

Under dark brows drawn into a straight line above his hawkish nose, she struggled to read his expression but made the obvious assumption he was worried she was going to fall apart. 'Don't worry. I'm not going to fall apart.'

It seemed to Beatrice that the present King

had decided to deal with her presence by directing every comment he made to a point six inches above her head. For some reason Beatrice found it very funny.

Absence had not made the King any less angry than she remembered. Her glance drifted from father to son, where Dante sat with his head bent attentively to catch what the person on his left was saying.

Despite her experience of a toxic stepfather, she had known what a *proper* father should be like. How could Dante know when all he had was his own father, who was a distant, cold figure, to go by?

What sort of father would Dante make?

It was a question she had asked herself the first time around, and it had bothered her because she simply couldn't see him that way. But now? Her eyes flickered wide as she realised how surprisingly easy it was to see him in that role. Had he changed, or was it the way she saw him, thought of him, that had altered?

What did they say? Expect the worst and hope for the best? Actually, against all expectations, this evening was not so bad, as her experience of official engagements went.

A fact in large part due to the conversation she'd struck up with one of the guests of honour, who protocol decreed had been seated to her right.

The ambassador's wife, an elegant young thirty-something Frenchwoman, who Beatrice soon discovered was a new parent and self-confessedly besotted.

'Sorry, I must be boring you. We have very little conversation between night feeds, teething and the general brilliance of our son,' she admitted, glancing fondly to where her husband was holding a stilted conversation with the Queen.

'I'm not bored.' Beatrice grinned and lowered her voice. 'But if you get onto the best vintage this decade to lay down for an investment... I might doze off,' she admitted with a twinkle as she glanced to the retired general seated on her left, who was giving all his attention to his glass of red.

It was refreshing to be around someone who was so obviously happy. Maybe it would rub off, she thought wistfully. 'Did you have Alain here?' she asked. The opening of the new maternity wing of the hospital had been one of her last official duties, frustrating as usual because her expressed wish to speak to some staff and patients without the photographers had been vetoed. 'Or did you go back home?'

'Oh, I didn't give birth. I can't actually have children. We adopted.'

At the opposite end of the table Dante was conscious that several people had begun to eavesdrop on the young women's conversation, though they themselves seemed unaware of the fact. It was as if people were shocked that nobody had told the women that this event was business, not pleasure.

'Really? My parents adopted too.'

As Beatrice's voice floated across the table, he was aware of his mother looking tenser by the moment.

The ambassador leaned across; he was smiling. 'Thank you.'

Dante lifted his brows.

'These formal events are a trial for Lara— she finds them something of an ordeal... The Princess has drawn her out.'

Dante was aware of something like proprietorial pride breaking loose inside him as he nodded, and found himself wondering how differently things might have worked out if his family had decided to consider Beatrice's natural warmth and genuine interest in people a positive rather than a handicap.

And you threw that warmth away. So, what does that make you?

Maybe it was true that you didn't value

what you had until it was no longer there, but now she was there, and he was determined that she would stay. She was the mother of his child; her place was with him. It was an explanation that he could live with. It meant he didn't have to delve too deeply into his tightly boxed emotions.

'Listen to them.' The ambassador's voice cut into Dante's bitter reflections.

Dante was, as were several other people who had tuned into the animated conversation between the two attractive women.

'So you're adopted?'

'No, my sister was adopted. My mum and dad had given up on getting pregnant by that point. They adopted Maya as a newborn, then a couple of months later Mum discovered that I was not a grumbling appendix.'

Lara Faure laughed and clapped her hands.

'So, you are almost twins.'

'That's what we say, except definitely not identical. Maya is dark and petite and I'm…' her brows hit her blonde hairline '…*not*! The irony is that Mum is dark and petite. I take after our dad, who was tall and blond, before he went bald, so I hope I haven't inherited that from him.' Her hand went to her head, where her frequently disobedient hair appeared to be in place, before dropping. Her fingers curled around the stem of her water glass as she swirled the contents, giving the impression she was breathing in the scent of wine as she lifted it to her lips.

'Your hair is natural!' the Frenchwoman exclaimed, her envious glance on Beatrice's glossy head.

'I had some blue streaks when I was at school.' The admission freed a grin. 'And was a redhead for about five minutes. That's about the limit of my rebellion, but these days, yes, this is *au naturelle*.'

'How lucky. Mine costs me a fortune and far too many hours to maintain. I've forgotten what colour I actually was.' The woman patted her elegant head and gave a self-deprecating shrug. 'Your sister is the brunette, you said?'

Beatrice nodded.

'I always wanted a sister. I was an only child. We hope one day we will be able to give Alain a brother or sister…'

'Maya and I are best friends and sisters,' Beatrice said, her voice warm with affection as she thought of her sister. 'We squabble, but I know…' She paused, becoming belatedly aware that the table had grown silent and that everyone was listening to every word she said. Well, too late to stop now, even though she knew she'd strayed onto a dangerous subject area. 'I know that she is always there for me.' She put down her glass and kept her eyes steadily on the woman beside her and imagined the thought bubbles of disapproval above the collective regal heads.

'And I'm sure you have always been there for her. You know, I have a few friends coming for brunch next week, you might know some? We have started up a book club, and on the side we have some pet projects at the moment. You might know that I am…was a violinist before the arthritis…?'

She briefly extended a hand displaying swollen knuckles while in a sentence she dismissed an unfair roll of the dice that had robbed her of a short but glittering career, and the world of someone considered one of the greats in the music industry.

Her bravery was humbling, and Beatrice knew this was someone she would like to know.

'They have a great system in place here for music in schools—an innovation of your husband, according to my sources?'

Beatrice said nothing, aware that the other woman's sources were a lot better than her own.

'But the younger appreciation of music

starts, the better, so we are hoping to raise some money for instruments to introduce music lessons into the nurseries in a fun way.'

'That sounds great,' Beatrice began, her smile deepening as she realised that she'd made a friend.

'Though I should warn you, you might be bored. Two others of our group are new parents too and another is pregnant, so you might get a bit tired of all the baby talk.'

Beatrice could not control the guilty colour she felt rising up her neck, even though she knew logically that nobody was about to suspect the truth. As far as anyone else was concerned they had been estranged for the last eight months and, while there might be a lot of speculation as to why she was back, a baby was not going to be on their list of possibilities.

As she continued to struggle to frame a response, aware that Lara was beginning to look puzzled by her silence, it was Dante who came to her rescue.

'Hands up.'

He held up his hands, the long tapering fingers splayed in an attitude of mea culpa that caused conversation to halt and every eye to turn his way. 'My fault.'

Beatrice's initial relief was immediately

tempered with wariness. What was he going to say?

Lara Faure raised a delicate brow, her teasing eyes flashing between the handsome Prince and his wife. 'It is in my experience that it is always the husband's fault.'

Beatrice held her breath as she waited for Dante to speak. The gleam in his dark eyes as they brushed her reminded her of the Dante she had fallen in love with, the Dante who made the outrageous sound normal, and had delighted in making her blush in public.

'I have been complaining,' he drawled, leaning back in his seat while his long, sensitive brown fingers now played an invisible tune on the white linen as they lightly drummed, 'that she spreads herself too thin—she has just so much *enthusiasm*.' His shoulders lifted in an expressive, fluid shrug. 'It makes her take on too many things. I have to book an appointment to see her.' He threw the words out, along with a heavy-lidded caressing look that sent Beatrice's core temperature up by several degrees.

Ignoring her burning blood, she focused on his ability to lie through his beautiful teeth and continued to conceal her true thoughts behind an impassive mask.

'Books and music. Two of her favourite

things.' And both offering no physical danger that might harm mother or child. 'Though I have to warn you, she can't hold a tune. I can spare you, *cara*, go have fun.'

'He likes to think I actually need to ask his permission before I have fun.'

People laughed and conversations started up, but under her own smile there was hope as she allowed herself to think that this was not all pretence.

CHAPTER ELEVEN

To Beatrice's relief the party did not drag on long after the meal. The guests of honour excused themselves relatively early and Dante took the opportunity to extract them at the same time.

As they walked through the doors into their private drawing room, he was tugging off his tie. A moment later the top buttons of his formal shirt were unfastened, and he gave a grunt of satisfaction before he flopped onto one of the deeply upholstered sofas that were arranged around the carved fireplace.

'That could have been worse.' He threw several cushions on the floor with a grimace of irritation before angling a glance at Beatrice. 'You don't agree?'

'Your father ignored me regally all evening.'

'I'd pay to have my father ignore me.'

She failed to fight off a smile.

'So what else?'

'I wanted to tell Lara that I was pregnant.'

'Then why didn't you?'

She slung him an exasperated look. 'I may know very little about royal protocols but I'm *pretty* sure telling a dinner guest I'm pregnant before the King and Queen know they are going to have a grandchild might break a couple.'

'True…but you have made a friend?'

'I like her,' she said, ignoring the invitation when he patted the arm of the sofa beside him and choosing to sit instead opposite, with the long coffee table, with the tasteful stack of prerequisite coffee-table books that nobody was ever going to read, between them.

Her eyes went to the hand that still rested on the arm as she wondered uneasily if the gesture had been meant to remind her of another occasion when she had accepted the invitation only to find herself pulled down on top of him. She pushed away the images, but not before her core temperature had jumped several uncomfortable degrees.

'Should I have told Lara that I'd join her book club?'

'Why not? You make it sound as though you've signed your soul away. And it sounds more like a mother and baby group and you will fit right in. I have a list of the obstetricians I spoke of, if you'd like to look at them.' He scanned her face. 'We can tell my parents, if that would make you feel more comfortable.'

'But what if something goes wrong?' The words 'like the last time' hung unspoken in the airwaves between them. She shook her head, the imagined scenes of that eventuality lodged there, a nightmare mixture of their lost baby and the emotionally charged scenes that had followed her mum's unsuccessful IVF attempts.

'You cannot think that way. You need to enjoy this pregnancy and you won't if you spend the entire time anticipating a problem.' She could leave that to him, he decided as he experienced a swell of helplessness, a reminder of the way he had felt when the first pregnancy had tragically ended.

He hadn't known what to do, what to say, and anything he had said had sounded trite and inadequate. He'd felt utterly helpless to lessen the grief she'd been feeling and unwilling to examine his own grief; his conditioning had kicked in and he'd taken refuge in work.

He knew he had failed her and was determined he would not again. He could keep her safe and he would.

'And if there is a problem?'

'Then we will deal with it together.'

It sounded good but it was the part he left out that made her look away. If anything went wrong with this pregnancy there would be no reason for her to be here.

'You know what would make you feel better?'

She forced a smile and tried to ease the sadness away. 'I'm pretty sure you're going to tell me.'

'You need to brush up on your lying skills, because you really are a terrible liar.'

'You make it sound like that is a bad thing.'

'A good lie gets you out of many a sticky situation, and sincerity,' he said, 'is a very bad thing, diplomatically speaking. Of course, if you can feign it—' He reached out and caught one of her shoes before it hit him in the face.

'I wasn't aiming at you.'

'Then you have real potential. That's better,' he approved when she lost her battle to contain her mirth.

'If you wore heels you'd know they are not a subject for jokes.'

'You don't need heels, and I already struggle with door frames,' he said, watching her wriggle her toes as she stretched out her legs towards the coffee table. He registered the tiny smile playing around the corners of her mouth before, tongue between her teeth, she nudged the neatly arranged books with her outstretched foot, spoiling their geometrical precision.

With effort he prised his eyes from the long length of her endless smooth legs. It did nothing to ease the pulsing need that had settled like a hot stone in his groin.

'Feel better now?'

'A little.'

'Sometimes saying what you want to is a luxury.'

His voice held no discernible inflection but something in his expression made her wonder if they were still talking book clubs. She somehow doubted it; the gleam she could see through the dark mesh of his lashes confirmed it.

The slow, heavy pump of her heart got louder in her ears. It was something that would be reckless to pursue, better leave it be.

Sound advice.

'What do you want to say?'

Playing with fire, Bea.

For a long moment he said nothing. 'Do you really want to know?'

She swallowed, frustrated at having the ball thrown back in her court. If she wanted this to go to the next level, he was saying she had to take the conscious step to make it happen... She'd have no one to blame but herself.

This was exactly the sort of situation she had sworn to avoid and here she was virtually running after it, running after him. She could feel that reckless *let tomorrow take care of itself* feeling creeping up on her. Even from this distance she could hear him breathing like someone who had just crossed the marathon finish line, or was that her?

Without taking his eyes off her, he levered himself into a sitting position, leaned across the table that separated them and ran a hand down the instep of one of her bare feet.

She sucked in a fractured breath, opened her mouth to say— She would never know what, because the phone that lay in the small beaded evening bag she had dumped on the table rang.

'Leave it!' he growled out as the noise shattered the moment.

Yanked back to reality and her senses and not nearly as grateful as she ought to be for the fact, Beatrice shook her head, pulled her feet back, tucking them under her as she delved into the bag. Pulling her phone out, she glanced at the screen.

'It's Maya. I have to take it.'

Dante's jaw clenched, all of him clenched as frustration pumped through his veins in a steady stream. 'Of course you do.' He doubted Beatrice heard him as she was already sweeping into the direction of the bedroom, her phone pressed to her ear.

When she returned a few minutes later Beatrice wasn't sure if Dante would still be there, then she saw him looking tall and dangerous, prowling up and down the room like a caged tiger, glass of something amber in his hand and the lamplight shading his impossibly high carved cheekbones.

'Maya says hello.'

He flashed her a look. 'I'm quite sure that's not what she said, but hello, Maya.' He raised his glass in a salute.

Beatrice's lips compressed as she glared at him. His continued pacing was really beginning to wind her up. As if she weren't already tense enough, and *guilty*.

Maya had to have picked up that she couldn't wait to get off the phone. Her concerned sister, whose only crime was to have bad or good timing, depending on how you looked at it.

She winced as she replayed the short conversation in her head. The gratitude she ought to have felt for being saved from basically herself was absent. The problem being she wasn't sure that she'd wanted to be saved.

Who was she kidding? She definitely hadn't wanted to be saved.

He halted his relentless pacing, drained his glass and set it down. It didn't take the taint of guilt and regret from his mouth. It seemed insane now that he had ever thought he could handle the scent of her perfume, the sound of her voice. It was all part of his personal agony. Wanting her was driving him out of his mind; the lust was all-consuming—it wiped out every other consideration.

He was still the same person; his own needs always would take priority.

'I can't say I blame her.'

Beatrice felt emotion swell in her chest. He sounded tired…and while you couldn't consider someone who was six feet five of solid bone and muscle vulnerable, his defences seemed to have lowered. Whatever internal battle he was fighting might have lowered his defences, but the dangerous explosive quality that was innate to him was much closer to the surface.

'Maya has nothing against you.'

His eyes lifted and he smiled; it held no humour. 'Of course she doesn't.'

'It's true, she is…protective, that's all.'

'I get that, and I admire her for it. I admire you. You are both there for each other,' he said broodingly.

She watched as he set his glass down with a thud and reached for the brandy.

'We're sisters, that's what it's like. You know that, you have a brother.'

The moment the words left her lips she knew she'd said the wrong thing.

She could almost smell the adrenalin coming off him as he stalked towards her, stopping a foot or so away. She couldn't take her eyes off the muscle clenching and unclenching in his hollow cheek.

'I was never there for my brother!' The words came out, acrid with self-loathing.

The confusion swirling in her head deepened. She took a step towards him and laid a hand on his forearm, conscious as she did so of the quivering coiled tension in the muscle that was iron hard.

It didn't cross her mind to be afraid or even nervous; she had never been afraid of Dante.

'But you are, Dante. You are doing all this.' She gestured to the room they stood in. 'For

Carl, you walked away from your life and you never blamed him once.'

'You think I am noble…that is so far from the truth, *cara*, that it is almost funny. I had no idea that he was gay, let alone that he was so unhappy.'

'Perhaps he wasn't ready to share.'

'I should have known,' Dante persisted stubbornly. 'What sort of brother doesn't know his brother is hating his life, is so unhappy?'

'Oh, Dante, I'm so sorry. But that is not your fault.'

'If I'd been any sort of brother, he would have felt able to come to me. He couldn't, he didn't. What sort of brother, man, does that make me?' He glanced down, seeming to notice for the first time the small hand on his arm.

He pushed it away and Beatrice, the hand he had rejected pressed up to her chest, stood there, absorbing his words. Her heart twisting in her chest for him, she felt helpless to ease the haunted guilt she could see shining in his dark eyes, but she knew she had to try.

'It's not your fault he was unhappy, but you could never make the decision for him, Dante. He had to find the courage in himself to do that, and he did.'

'Oh, yeah, I was a really great person to confide in,' he sneered. 'My brother was crying out for help, a silent scream, but I was too busy with my own life. I did what all certified selfish bastards do. I looked after number one.'

His anguish felt like a dull blade in her heart.

This time when she laid a hand on his arm, he didn't shrug it off.

'Have you spoken to Carl about this?' she asked, wary of putting too much pressure on him. 'Asked him how he feels? Told him how *you* feel?' Her hand slid down his forearm until it covered his hand, her fingers sliding in between his.

She already knew the answer to that. Dante was not a man who spoke about feelings, which made her sure that it would not be long before he was regretting sharing this much with her.

'We don't talk about it,' he said, thinking of the email that remained on his phone. His brother had said all he needed in that, and neither of them had referred to it since.

'Maybe you should…' She paused, her heart aching as she saw the guilt that was eating him up. 'Talk? Maybe *we* should talk too?'

'I've always lived for myself. I can't be the man…your—'

'You are my man, my husband.'

'What are you doing, Bea?' The pupils of his eyes expanded dramatically as his glance rested on his own hand, now caught between both of hers, as she raised it to her mouth and touched his fingertips with her lips.

She felt muscles bunch in rejection and let go of his hand, but only in order to reach up and grab the back of his neck, dragging his face down to enable her to slant her lips across his.

She wanted to say, *Here is my heart, Dante, let me love you*, but instead she said, 'Make love to me, Dante.'

It was a fight he was always going to lose.

He had no idea how long it lasted before a groan that reverberated through his body was wrenched from his throat as he dragged her to him.

One hand behind the back of her head, he covered her mouth with his, the heat an explosion as their lips touched, their tongues tangled. The passion released burnt everything but raw need away.

The only cool he was aware of was the feel of her hands on his skin as she pushed her hands under the fabric of his shirt, across his chest and down over his belly, causing him to suck in gasps and then groans of en-

it hit she was not broken, but miraculously whole again. She lost herself in the feeling as wave after wave of pleasure rippled along every individual nerve ending in her body.

After it ended, and he lay breathing hard on top of her, responding to a primal need to extend this intimacy, she wrapped her arms around his waist and whispered fiercely, *'Stay,'* against the damp skin of his neck.

He kissed her and pulled her head onto his chest and they lay, still joined, until she felt him stir inside her.

Her wide eyes flicked to his face so close to her own.

'You make me hungry, *cara.'*

'You make me greedy.'

Later that night they made love again, slower and with infinite tenderness, exploring each other's bodies with an endless fascination. The lightest touch of his hand and mouth made her body vibrate with pleasure. She sobbed with the intensity of it and every touch was heightened by the shattering depth, the sheer *intensity* of emotions that accompanied each brush of her skin.

When the deep release came it took her a long time to float back to earth.

Did she say, 'I love you,' over and over as she sobbed or was that part of a dream?

Beatrice was not sure.

Dante did not sleep. Beatrice lay sleeping in his arms. His heart contracted when he looked at the perfect beauty of her face. It was hard feeling what he did when he looked at her, to hold on to the lie he told himself that what they shared was just sex, but it would never be *just* anything with Beatrice. He might try and deny it but deep down he had always known that. He felt a fool that he had ever imagined he could treat Beatrice like other women. She had always been different, she had always made him feel… Jaw clenched, he blocked the thought process before it led him to a place he was not ready to go, a truth he was not ready to see.

A man could change; she had made him believe that, because against all the odds she believed in him. As he looked down at the woman lying like a sleeping angel in his arms, he vowed to deserve her faith.

CHAPTER TWELVE

IT WAS STILL dark when Dante sliding away from her woke Beatrice. She stretched and stopped, the memories that explained the stiffness of her muscles flooding back. She reached out in the dark, her hand touching the smooth warm skin of his back.

Seated on the edge of the bed, he responded to her sleepy murmur of protest with a kiss that deepened as her lips softened beneath the pressure before he pulled away abruptly.

Suddenly cold even though the air was warm, she shivered.

'Who has a conference call in the middle of the night?' she complained, raising herself on one elbow and pushing the silky skein of hair from her sleepy eyes, desire ribboning through her and settling heavy and low in her abdomen as she smelt him on her skin.

'The half of the world that has been awake

hours. It is what living in a global economy is all about, and it is not night...'

He heard her reach out for the lamp and covered her hand with his. 'No, leave it.' If he saw her, read the sultry invitation in her eyes and remembered feeling the aftershocks of her climax as they'd stayed joined as one, he was pretty sure that he would never get to that call.

She ignored him—of course she did.

She looked every bit as wanton and glorious as he had imagined as she sat there, her perfect breasts partially concealed by her hair.

She pouted. 'I don't want to be awake.' She didn't want the night to end; she knew it would, she just didn't want to think about it yet.

He slanted a kiss across her lips, the touch making her shiver, and flicked off the light.

'Then go back to sleep.'

It was a week later that Dante walked into the drawing room just as a young woman was walking out. This was the second time this week he had managed to arrange his day to include lunch with Beatrice.

On one level he couldn't believe he was trying to earn brownie points from his own wife, but amazingly he actually found that his new schedule made him more productive.

'Who was that?'

'My new PA.'

His eye-framing dark brows lifted. 'You are not letting the grass grow under your feet.'

'She came highly recommended.'

'By whom?'

'Jacintha.'

His brow furrowed as he loosened his tie. 'Who is Jacintha, again?'

'The maid. The one with the red hair and cool glasses.'

'You hired a PA on the say-so of a maid?'

'Should I have run it past you?' she challenged.

'Not at all.'

She smiled. 'Well, Jacintha's recommendation, and those of her previous employers.' She gave a small smug smile as she listed them, watching his eyes widen. 'I know working for me does seem like a step down, but she wants to come home because her mother has a heart condition. The best thing is she is not related even by marriage to any of *the* families.' It did not take long to figure out that most of the top positions in the palace were given to relatives or cronies of a handful of historically powerful San Macizan families.

'This will cause a storm in a champagne glass, you know that?' he mused, watching her face with a half-smile as he perched on the edge of the polished mahogany desk and began to leaf through the diary that lay open. 'Wow, you have hit the ground running,' he remarked as he skimmed through the entries written in her distinctive hand. 'Oh, leave Tuesday morning free. I've made an appointment with the obstetrician and—' He stopped and leaned in closer as he reread the most recent entry that had caught his attention before he stabbed it with his finger. 'What is this?'

'What is what?' she asked, not understanding the ice in his voice.

'"Fun run, five K, fancy dress optional",' he read out.

'Oh, that's Lara. She rang earlier. She is organising a fun run for the children's hospice. I agreed to take part.'

'That is out of the question.' The diary closed with a decisive click and he was on his feet looking tall, austere, and oozing simmering disapproval while inside his gut was churning with visceral fear.

She clung to her temper and reminded herself that this fragile peace between them required concessions on both sides. 'I don't have to wear fancy dress.'

'Running five K is a reckless risk in your condition.'

Her lips tightened as she pushed out her chin to an aggressive angle and, hands on her hips, stalked towards him, stopping a couple of feet away. 'There is nothing reckless about it. It is basically a fun jog or walk for a good cause, and I will enjoy it!'

'The risk is too great.'

Struggling to channel a calm she was not feeling, Beatrice held his stormy gaze. 'Do you really think that I would risk the life of our child on a whim?'

His eyes slid from her own, his chest lifting, before returning as he growled out reluctantly, 'No. The last time—'

The shadow of fear she glimpsed in this strong, seemingly invulnerable man's eyes drained the anger from her. She hurt for him because he couldn't own that fear, he couldn't reach out. 'I'm scared too, Dante,' she confessed, tears standing out in her eyes. 'But I can't...'

Nostrils flaring, he looked down into her face and felt the anger and frustration drain away. 'I'm your husband. Why won't you let me protect you?'

'Protect, not suffocate.' She took his silence as encouragement and added, 'And I'll make my own appointment, choose my own doctor.'

'Shall I come back later?'

Dante stepped back and gestured towards the table under the window embrasure. 'No, that's fine,' he said to the maid, without taking his eyes from Beatrice's face. 'Put it on the table.'

'Shall I fetch another cup?'

'No!' Beatrice supplied as the door closed silently behind the scared-looking young maid. 'So, I'll tell Lara, no, you won't come to cheer me on, shall I? She figured that would be worth double in sponsorship.'

He dragged a hand through his dark hair, the internal struggle clear on the hard drawn lines on his handsome face. 'I will donate, and I'll come and support you.'

Her jaw dropped at the capitulation. 'You'll come.'

He shrugged. 'Someone has to make sure you don't decide to get competitive, but in return—'

'Return for what?' she began explosively before literally biting her tongue. 'In return what?'

'In return you go and see the doctor I made the appointment with. She is the best.'

Was it really a point worth making? She released a long hissing breath. 'All right.' She fixed him with a warning glance. 'But the next time you make a unilateral decision concerning me or the baby—don't!'

He gave a slow smile. 'I wouldn't dare.'

The walk through the private grounds calmed Beatrice after the confrontation. Gradually her pace slowed to a stroll as the healing of the quiet and solitude and nature's beauty seeped imperceptibly into her.

She remained, what? Wary, confused? Nobody in the universe made her *feel* as much as Dante did, and she couldn't get the fear she had seen in his eyes out of her head.

Instead of lunch with his wife, Dante spent a half hour pounding his body into submission in the private gym.

His mind remained another matter. Had he made the right decision? He knew that their marriage could not survive if they maintained a war of attrition. There had to be compromise even though it went against his instincts, and the idea of her running...falling... He threw himself into the next series of repetitions in the hope the pain in his muscles would drown out the torturous thought in his head.

Drenched with sweat, he was finally heading for the shower when he felt it.

Around him, weights in their cradles began to shake as the low distinctive subterranean growl of the earthquake built.

His first thought was Beatrice. He didn't pause. He grabbed his phone and got a low static buzz…and hit the ground running. Face set in grim lines, he was exiting the leisure facility when he encountered a uniformed figure who, without a word, fell into step beside him.

'We have set up a command centre in the old armoury to coordinate all rescue efforts.'

Dante nodded his approval. It made sense; the walls were ten feet thick and the building was cut into solid rock. 'Highness, we have choppers ready and waiting and the King and Queen will be evacuated as a priority. It's the communications that are the problem.'

'I'm on that…'

'My wife?'

'She left by the south-west door, heading in the direction of the sunken garden, twenty minutes ago.'

Lifting a finger in acknowledgement, Dante picked up his pace, leaving the military figure behind.

Bea dropped the flower she had just picked and froze, trying to figure out if she was having a dizzy spell or... The answer to her question came in the form of a deep primal subterranean roar that went on and on, it felt like for hours. She wasn't swaying but the ground was.

It stopped, and there was a total silence. Not even a bird sang or a bee buzzed, then, as if a switch had been flicked, individual sounds began to emerge from the silence. The noise built; there were cries from all directions mingling with the distant sound of sirens.

Beatrice hadn't moved; there'd just been an earthquake. What did she do, stay outside or go indoors? The sounds were mostly coming from the buildings.

She was still standing in frozen indecision when a familiar figure wearing running shorts and a gym vest appeared. She let out a sigh of relief. Dante was here; things would be all right. It might be illogical when you were dealing with the forces of nature, but she believed it. But he didn't know she was there.

Tears ran down her face as she tried to cry out, but nothing came, then, it was a miracle, just before he would have vanished from her eyeline, he turned.

A moment later he was racing towards her.

His name was lost in the warmth of his mouth as he grabbed her by the shoulders and dragged her into him. Crushing her as he kissed her with the hunger of a starving man.

When the kiss stopped, he lifted his head. 'Beatrice, you're safe…you're safe… Oh, God!' he groaned, dragging his hands down either side of her face, framing her delicate features, a mixture of frustration and fascination stamped on his face.

'I want…this is…' Teeth clenched, he set her away from him. 'We experienced an earthquake.' Unable to take his eyes off her, he ran his hands up and down her arms as he scanned her face. 'There may be aftershocks. You can't be here. Are you hurt?'

She shook her head. 'No, I'm fine. So that was an earthquake.'

'Yes.'

He sounded very calm and maybe it was catching because she could breathe again without panting. 'I'm scared.'

'Yes.'

'I want to help…'

'No—no, you don't.'

Hands on her shoulders, he led her firmly back in the direction she had just come into the open green space of the gardens. He pushed her down on a stone bench and squatted down beside her.

'Listen carefully. I have to go,' he admitted, frustration etched in the strong lines of his face. 'But I won't be long. You stay here and if… There might be aftershocks and if there are, just get under this.' He patted the bench. 'You'll be safe, and I'll be back.'

She nodded. 'Be careful.'

Already feet away and jogging, he turned and grinned over his shoulder, waving a hand as though he were off for his morning run.

An hour later, Dante was relieved to see Bea sitting in the same place he had left her, but she seemed to have been joined by a dog.

The dog gave a warning growl when he approached, then licked his hand when he offered it. By the time he knelt beside Beatrice they were best friends.

'He just appeared,' she said, adding urgently, 'The earthquake, Dante?'

'So, right, first indications are it's not too bad.'

'Thank goodness!' She hadn't really been

conscious of how high her tension levels were until they lowered, leaving her knees literally shaking as she reached out to stroke the fawning dog.

'What does not too bad mean?' she pressed cautiously as he pulled himself to his feet. It was weird that she loved the fluid grace of his movements, even at a time like this.

'Riota had the worse of it.'

She nodded, knowing that the only things on the uninhabited rocky outcrop a mile off the coast were the native tough sheep who, it had been explained, were ferried out there each breeding season and brought back after lambing.

'The damage is concentrated on the east coast.'

She released another little gusty sigh. It was another area where the rugged terrain meant there were no settlements.

'There was a landslip so the coast road is blocked, which is causing some problems. As far as I can tell from reports, the damage to outlying areas is minimal and, though there have been a few minor injuries, nothing significant so far. Except, of course, I'm sure it feels significant for the people involved. I need to get to Mentsa. The emergency services are coping but there is some panic. The church tower there has fallen.

'We're still assessing the airport, but the helicopter that dropped Carl off has already taken my parents to the mainland, and a few essential—'

At the mention of his parents, she shook her head.

'I get it,' she said, struggling not to judge, but it was hard when you compared the powerful couple's apparent response to their son's. Dante's instinct was to protect his people and theirs was to protect themselves.

She struggled to subdue her anger—this was not the time or the place—but she was determined to point it out the next time they criticised anything Dante did—always assuming that she would be here to say anything.

The abrupt realisation brought with it a wave of desolation as, still playing mental catch-up, she dragged her wandering thoughts back to the present.

'Carl is here?'

'He was on the mainland.' He slid his foot into his boot and looked up, meeting her eyes. 'I followed your advice and we were going to meet up and talk in person. He jumped in a chopper as soon as he heard. He's persuaded

Grandfather to evacuate, along with you and some of the—'

Well, good luck with that, she thought. 'Along with me?' she interrupted.

Dante bent his head to tighten the belt on the trousers he had exchanged for his shorts. Nobody had produced a shirt; he still wore the vest that clung to the contours of his muscled chest and exposed the powerful musculature of his arms. He flashed her an impatient look.

'Don't be difficult,' he pleaded.

'I thought you said there is no danger.'

'There isn't.'

She gave an eloquent shrug and stood her ground.

'I'll just have someone gather a few essentials for you and be ready in five minutes. Someone will—'

'I've only just got back. I'm not going anywhere.' This was so frustrating; she had so much she needed to say. 'Are *you* leaving?'

He stood with his phone half raised to his ear. 'I'll be fine.'

'I have no doubt,' she countered coolly. 'That wasn't what I asked.'

'Me leave!'

He looked so offended by the mere suggestion and for a moment the surge of warmth and love she felt for this man swamped everything else she was feeling.

'That would hardly send out the right message. Panic is the problem. My presence will hopefully help keep a lid on things. What are you doing? The helicopters are waiting. You need to get going and I need...' *You*, he thought and shooed the thought away.

She swallowed. 'You're hurt.' She walked up to him and touched the graze on his cheek that was seeping blood.

He moved back from her touch, a spasm of dismissal twisting his lips; he could not afford any distractions. 'It is nothing. You need to hurry.' He caught her wrists and looked down at her, allowing himself the indulgence for a moment of drinking in her lovely face.

'Your grandfather isn't going to go quietly.' Yet another worry for his already overburdened, though very broad, shoulders to bear.

Dante fought the reluctance to release her wrists and stepped back. 'He's a stubborn old— But don't worry,' he added, moderating his tone. 'We'll make sure he's all right.'

'Yes, I know you will,' she said, shaking back her hair and gathering it in one hand with a practised double twist of her wrist, then securing it in a haphazard ponytail on the base of her neck. 'So, what do you want me to do?'

He stared at her as though she were talking a foreign language. 'What are you talking about, Beatrice? I really don't have the time for you to— How am I supposed to focus if I'm worried about you?'

'I'm not going.'

'Beatrice...!'

'How about I trust you to take care of yourself, and you trust me? I can absolutely promise you that I have no intention of putting myself in harm's way,' she said, standing there with a protective hand pressed to her stomach.

After a moment of silence, she saw the flash of something in his eyes before he tipped his head in silent acknowledgement.

'I haven't got time for this.'

'That's what I was counting on,' she admitted and drew a grin that briefly lightened the sombre cast of his expression.

'All right. I'm staying, you're staying. But if you—'

She waved her hand in a gesture of impatience. 'Get under your feet? Faint? I get it. As always, your opinion of me is flattering,' she observed drily. 'Just go do your stuff, Dante.'

He stood there, his body clenched as duty warred with instinct. His instinct was telling him to carry her, kicking and screaming if necessary, to safety. His duty was to keep everybody safe, but how could he do that if he didn't know Beatrice was safe? His normal ability to compartmentalise deserted him in the moment as he looked down at her. Despite his terror at the thought of her and their child coming to harm, a terror that only increased when he imagined not being there for her, his eyes glowed with admiration.

The next time anyone said anything about genes he would tell the bastards that his wife knew more about the meaning of service and duty than the rest of his family put together!

Still he hesitated, unwilling, unable, to leave her, all his instincts telling him it was his job to protect her.

'Is that my protection detail?' she said, as three uniformed figures appeared on the horizon.

He nodded. 'Do as they tell you.'

'I will.'

She saw him exchange words with the approaching detail as their paths crossed, but they were too distant for her to hear what was said.

All three of the tough-looking military

types, not seeming breathless even though they'd been running, paused with brief formality to bow when they reached her.

One stepped up. 'Highness, we are—' He broke off and, one hand pressed to his earpiece, turned away, listening.

'Is there a problem?' Beatrice asked anxiously.

The men exchanged glances, as though asking each other if it was appropriate to respond.

'My husband…?'

'His Highness will have received the information. It is confirmation that the palace has escaped any real structural damage, so it is safe to return. Actually the first reports suggest that there is very little structural damage at all, but there has been a partial wall collapse.'

'Inside the palace?' Beatrice asked.

He nodded. 'The nursery.'

The fine muscles around her mouth quivered. There were still wisps of panic floating through her head, but she was able to speak like a relatively calm person even if inside felt a lot less confident of her ability to cope.

'Are there casualties?' she asked, her thoughts quickly moving past her insecurities to the children she had seen on a visit earlier that week. She felt her eyes fill and blinked away the moisture as she pushed the now poignant memories away.

Tears were not going to help. Tears were for later, hopefully along with smiles. Right now she needed to focus.

'By some miracle it seems not.'

The tears she had tried to suppress spilled out, along with a laugh of sheer relief.

'Apparently they were all in the playground. There are scrapes and cuts, all minor, and a hell of a lot of hysterical parents arriving. The emergency services are having a lot of trouble. We need to keep them in one place. They need to take a headcount, but it's like— and I quote—"*herding cats*", which makes it really hard for them to assess the situation.'

'The headmistress struck me as pretty competent. Is she still there?'

'She is concussed and has been hospitalised, so the main priority is to move the children and parents out of the immediate area without losing track of any children, so that we can secure the building against any potential aftershocks. It sounds simpler than it is. It's pandemonium.'

'But someone is helping.'

'Us, once you are safe, Highness.'

She held up a hand and wished she possessed half the calm she was channelling. 'Why waste time? Take me with you.'

The military figure shook his head. 'Our instructions are to—'

'I'm giving you new instructions. What's the harm? You said it's safe.'

CHAPTER THIRTEEN

Dante was on the way to the airport, which luckily had suffered no damage, and he was speaking to his brother via speakerphone.

'I should get there before your flight leaves. Do you have to fly straight out?'

'I've got a meeting I can't get out of to-morrow.'

'Right. I should make it before your flight if there are no hold-ups.'

'Is your heroine wife with you?'

'Heroine… Beatrice, you mean?'

'You got any other wives? They are playing the video on the big screens and there's not a dry eye in the house. She had all the kids singing and she's carrying the little guy—'

Dante could feel the pressure build in his temples as he tried to speak. He managed to get the words past his clenched lips on the third attempt. 'Beatrice is at the nursery, the one where the wall collapsed?' The news of a successful evacuation had reached him but not that his wife was involved in the process.

'Well, she was earlier, but the parents are being interviewed now and all are singing her praises. You're going to have to name a park after her, or put up a statue or something.'

Dante, who did not connect with the amusement in his brother's voice, swore loud and fluently, cutting his brother off mid-flow. He brought the car around in a vicious one-hundred-and-eighty-degree turn that sent up a dust cloud of gravel, and floored the gas pedal.

Beatrice spent a luxurious half hour in a hot shower, washing off the accumulated dirt and grime. Dressed in a blue silk robe, her long wet hair wrapped in a towel twisted into a turban, she walked back into the bedroom. She had checked her phone sixty seconds ago but she checked it again. Nothing since the missed call earlier, but the mobile mast had been down for a good part of the day and there were numerous black spots on the is-land.

She sighed. At times like this a fertile imagination was not a friend. She knew that she wouldn't be able to relax until she had contact from Dante again.

She walked over to the mirror, untwisted the turban and began to pat her long hair dry. She had picked up a brush to complete the task when the door burst open.

Dante stood there, his tall, lean frame filling the doorway, wearing fatigue pants that clung to his narrow hips; the vest that might once have been white was stained with dust and dirt. His dark skin seemed liberally coated with the same debris.

Relief flooded through her as her face broke into a smile of dizzy relief. 'Dante!' She was halfway across the room when she realised that something was very wrong. 'Are you hurt? Has something happ—'

'Quite a lot, it seems.'

She stopped dead. She could hear the flame pushing against the ice in his voice, and literally feel the raw emotion pulsing off him.

'I asked you to stay safe, I asked you... You promised, and what do you do?' He advanced a step towards her and paused, close enough now for her to see the muscle throbbing in his lean cheek. 'I trusted you to take care of yourself and our baby and then what do I discover? That you decided to put yourself and...and our child straight in the path of danger, quite deliberately.'

She gulped. 'The nursery, you mean? There

was no danger. It was just, just…herding cats, that was all.'

'You could have died,' he rasped hoarsely.

She looked at this strange, coldly furious Dante and fell back on defiance. 'You could die crossing the road.'

A hissing sound left his white clenched lips.

'I told you to stay safe.'

Her chin lifted. 'And I made my own judgement.'

'You put our child in danger.'

'How dare you?' she cried, surging towards him, her hands clenched into fists, not sure in the moment if the anger fizzing up inside her was directed at the insulting accusation or the fact he was confirming that that was what this was about. It wasn't her safety; it was the baby. It was always about the baby, this time and last time.

Suddenly she was angry with herself as much as him for wanting to believe differently, wanting to believe she was more than a means to an end, a person, not an incubator.

He watched as, hands outstretched, she backed away from him, her chest heaving.

'How dare you even suggest that?' she began, her low, intense voice building in volume with each successive syllable. 'You are the father. Does it make you a bad father for putting yourself in danger today? No, that makes you a man doing the right thing. Well, I did the right thing today too. Women do not stay at home waiting for the heroes' return and knitting socks these days…my child was never in any danger at any point!'

Unable to stop seeing her body crushed beneath a pile of rubble, her dead eyes looking up at him, the nightmare vision playing on a loop in his head, he barely registered what she was saying.

'If it wasn't for the baby…' *for me*, the voice in his head condemned '…you wouldn't even be here today.' In danger and it was all down to him. He hadn't been there for her; he had never been there for her.

Just as he'd never been there for Carl.

She flinched as though he had struck her. 'I am aware of that,' she said, hugging the crushing hurt to herself. Did he think she needed that pointed out?

'Things need to change. Your safety is all that matters. You must come first.'

She stood there, knowing he meant the baby, but letting herself imagine for a moment how it might feel if the fierce protective emotion in his dark eyes was really for her, and when the moment passed she felt flat and empty. 'Some things you can't change.' You couldn't make someone love you and it was about time she started dealing with facts.

'I have to go.'

'Of course you do,' she said flatly.

'To the airport to say…things I need to say to my brother.'

'Well, don't expect me to be here when you get back because I'm going to keep my baby safe and I don't feel safe here, with you.' Like arrows, she aimed the words at his broad back.

Did he flinch at the impact? She didn't know, but she hoped so.

Dante got out of the car in front of the airport terminal and realised he didn't remember driving there at all. *Now that couldn't be a good thing, could it?*

As he strode in he glanced at the departure board. He had just caught his brother. He dodged some airport officials bearing down on him and tried not to notice a group sharing their experiences with a camera crew.

He almost made it.

'And here we have the Crown Prince himself, who was in the thick of it,' an enterprising journalist said, shoving a microphone in his face. 'Would you say this has been a lucky escape, sir?' He started to trot as it became obvious that Dante was not slowing down. 'The buildings here are pretty robust.'

'And the people,' Dante responded, walking on.

'The rebuilding,' the guy called after him.

Rebuilding. Dante's pace slowed for the first time as the scene with Beatrice flashed before his eyes. He had not rebuilt; he had demolished the progress they had made in a matter of minutes.

Carl, who was scanning a laptop that lay across his knees, looked up when Dante entered, closing the door on his bodyguard who stood outside. He set aside the computer and got up, walking straight across to his brother, wrapping him in a brotherly hug, which Dante returned.

Carl stepped back and, though half a head shorter than his younger brother, retained his grip on Dante's shoulders.

'Thank you for this.'

Carl looked bemused by the warm words. 'For what?'

'For coming back. And I'm sorry. I should have said it before, but I am truly.'

Carl shook his head. 'I hate to repeat myself, but for what?'

'For not being there for you. I *should* have had your back.'

Carl looked astonished. 'But you did.'

'I didn't know.'

'You were my younger brother. I couldn't burden you with my problems, with the emphasis on *"my"*. It took me a long time to get to that point. I was either going to accept the status quo or take that leap of faith, and you know me, I'm not like you. I was never one to put my head over the parapet and risk having it knocked off. I was the "toe the line for a quiet life" son.'

Though Dante looked thoughtful as he listened to this ruthless self-assessment, his expression and emotions were locked firmly in self-condemnation mode.

'I should have known how unhappy you were.'

'It wasn't about being unhappy. I was always just a wrong fit. I could never inspire the way you do. It's true!' Carl exclaimed when Dante shook his head, looking patently uncomfortable.

'This was always my decision to make and for a long time I wasn't brave enough.' His hand fell from his brother's shoulders. 'I'm happy I've met someone. And you have Beatrice back. How is the heroine?'

'I love her,' Dante said in a driven voice. He looked shocked. 'I love her,' he repeated slowly. 'Is this how it feels?' he asked, a kind of wonder in his voice. 'Oh, hell, I've been such an idiot.'

'Have you told her any of this?'

'She deserves better.'

'Than what?'

'Me! I'm a selfish bastard.'

'I have to tell you, brother, I prefer you as a bastard than a martyr. Maybe Beatrice does too,' he added slyly, and watched the hope flare in his brother's eyes.

'What are you doing?'

Beatrice gave a start and spun around, her blonde hair almost flaring out then settling in a silky curtain to her shoulder blades as she faced Dante, who stood with his broad shoulders propped against the wall beside the door.

Once she moved past the head-spinning blood rush of adrenalin that had her poised in 'deer in the headlights' mode, she realised that, though the anger he had been nursing earlier had gone, it had been replaced by an explosive quality. He made her think of a time bomb ticking down, every taut muscle and clenched sinew stretched to the limit.

'I've just been packing.'

'So, you're running away?'

She turned away as she felt her eyes fill. 'I'm moving rooms,' she contradicted. 'I'm not sure I could be termed essential travel. It's ironic. I can cope with the petty official and your family, but, you're right, I am leaving because I can't stay with a man who doesn't trust me. You're not wrapping me in cotton wool, you're suffocating me!'

He flinched. 'I know I said some unforgivable things but when I knew that you had been… I just went like ice inside. I felt terror, real gut-freezing terror. I haven't felt that way since you lost the baby. I felt so bloody helpless.'

Her eyes fluttered wide with shock.

'I could see the pain in your eyes and I didn't know what to say. I couldn't help you. It was the worst feeling of my entire life, seeing you hurt. And being the emotionally crippled mess-up I am, I had no words…' He made a sound of boiling frustration between his clenched teeth as she grabbed his head in both hands. 'I should have been able to make you feel better. I should have kept you safe. I failed you and this time… I cannot *bear* to see you go through that again.' He swallowed hard, and captured her eyes with his agonised gaze. 'I swore to myself that I'd keep you safe but all I've ended up doing is pushing you away—*again*!'

'I'm still here.'

He extended his hands towards her and after a moment she took them. 'Don't leave me, Beatrice. Stay with me.'

'I'm frightened too,' she whispered.

'But you are no coward. You are the bravest person I know, and now the world knows too. I am proud of you and even if there was no baby, I would love you.'

Her lips quivered as she looked up at him, drinking in the details of his marvellous face. 'I love you, Dante.'

He bent his head, the ferocious hunger of his kiss leaving her limp and ludicrously happy as he trailed a finger down the curve of her cheek. 'I adore you. I am half a man without you but—'

She pressed a finger to his lips; she was not interested in buts. She had heard all she needed to. 'I love you, Dante. I always have and I always will.'

He caught her hand, his eyes not leaving her face as he pressed it to his lips. 'I love you, Beatrice. I thought loving you meant letting you go free, but now I know that I can't make that choice for you. It is yours to make.'

Raising herself on tiptoes, she took his face

between her hands. 'I choose love.' She kissed him. 'I choose you.' She kissed him. 'I choose staying...say that again,' she said fiercely.

'What part?'

'The only part that matters, idiot. Say you love me!'

'I love you, Beatrice!'

She wound her arms around his neck, her feet leaving the floor as he kissed her back.

The kisses took them to the bed where, when they finally came up for air, they lay face to face, thigh to thigh, gazing into each other's eyes.

'I love your mouth,' she husked, exploring the individual dust-engrained lines on his face slowly, as if memorising them.

'Did Carl catch his flight?'

Dante nodded, unable to take his eyes off her face.

'And you two, are you okay?'

She was relieved when he nodded again.

'I'm glad.'

'So am I.'

'So what time is your parents' flight back?'

'They've delayed until tomorrow.' A sardonic smile twisted his lips. 'So the dust will literally have settled.' He slid a hand down her thigh and pulled it up and across his waist, dragging her in closer.

'This would be much better with no clothes.'

'It will be, but there is no hurry.'

She sighed and gave a sinuous wriggle closer, loving the hard lines of his body.

'I have a message for you from them.'

'Oh, don't spoil it!'

'They have asked me to inform you that it makes them very happy that you've returned. They are talking about a renewal of our vows.'

She felt her jaw drop. 'Is that some sort of joke?'

'No joke, they tell me you are *trending*...'

Her eyes flew wide. *'What?'*

'A photo of you has gone viral.'

He rolled far enough away to pull his phone from his pocket and scrolled to the photo that showed a golden-haired, jeans-clad Beatrice against a background of billowing dust, surrounded by a group of children who were all caught in the moment, looking up at her, while two of the smallest ones were thrown one over each shoulder. Dust particles caught by a ray of light made it seem as though she were surrounded by a shimmering golden glow.

After a slight hesitation she rolled forward, anchoring her hair from her face with her forearm. It afforded him a view of her face while she scanned the image that was the sort guaranteed to make a photographer's career.

It was no surprise to him that online fame did not seem to thrill her.

'Oh, God!'

'You don't look thrilled at the fame— *hashtag heroineprincess.*'

It took her a moment to recognise the moment someone had captured in an idealised version. The reality had involved dust and noise and a gut-wrenching sense of urgency as, afraid she would lose one of her charges, she'd tried to get them out of the exclusion zone around the unstable wall.

'It's embarrassing,' she countered, 'and I was not being brave. I was at my wits' end. It *was* like herding cats.'

'My parents are very impressed. They believe that you are an asset to the family, and, yes, that is a direct quote.'

Suddenly she was so angry she could barely breathe, let alone speak. When she finally made her vocal cords work, what her voice lacked in force it made up for in throbbing, furious sincerity. 'It really has nothing to do with them!'

'This is something I pointed out.'

She huffed out a tiny breath. 'Good!'

'They then informed me that it was my duty to save my marriage.'

'I hope you told them to stuff their duty!' she exploded.

'I did not use those words precisely, but that was the sentiment behind my response. I hate my life without you in it. It's a life with no heartbeat, no soul. I love you.' His gaze sank to the pulse pumping at the base of her throat. Her neck extended as he bent to kiss the pulse spot, his mouth moist against her hot skin.

'Because I'm an asset? Did they really say that? Should we tell them about the baby, do you think?'

The tentative question was lost on Dante. She was smiling into his eyes and he had never seen anything so beautiful in his life.

'I can't tell if I can hear your heartbeat or mine.'

'We have one, we are one. I love you, Beatrice. Being without you made me realise how much. Life without you is not a whole life. I'm not whole. I have a Beatrice-sized empty space inside me. When we married, I didn't know what love was,' he admitted. 'But you taught me how to love, and I know I will never love another woman. It isn't possible—we are two halves that make a whole.'

There were tears glimmering like diamonds in her eyes by the time he finished. 'I choose, I choose to be with you, always.'

'I love you, Beatrice. Stay with me, be my wife and let me be *me* with you, even if I have to be royal for the world.'

She flung her arms around his neck, grinning as tears streamed down her face. 'You'll never get rid of me, Dante, not now, not ever.'

Several moments later a maid walked in; her eyes flew wide as she saw the couple locked in a passionate embrace.

Within thirty minutes the entire palace knew the Princess they loved was home for good; there was a collective sigh of relief. They knew the couple was their future.

EPILOGUE

'CAN I HOLD HER?' Rachel Monk whispered.

Standing beside the open French doors that led onto a flower-filled balcony, Beatrice smiled at her mother, who stood there looking too young to be a grandmother in her bold emerald green dress coat, a jaunty hat and heels that showed off her great legs.

Carefully she gave the sleeping baby to her mother.

'Not much point being quiet with that lot down there.' The christening party was still in full swing.

'You know I am so proud of you, don't you… Bea?'

'And I'm proud of you.' Her mum's work with the charity for women in abusive relationships had won more than her own admiration.

They had both moved on from the past.

'I wish your father was here.'

'Oh, I think he is—have you seen that chin, the dimple?' she said, looking down fondly at her daughter's face. Everything else about Sabina Elsa was pure Dante. Her daughter was going to be a beauty.

'She is a miracle.'

Beatrice turned her head. 'What are you doing, creeping up on us like that?' she asked, looking up at her tall, gorgeous husband with smiling eyes. 'She *is* a miracle,' she added softly.

They would always grieve for their lost baby, but it was balanced by the joy that his or her sister had brought into their lives. They both knew how lucky they were; they told each other so every day.

'Say cheese!'

They both turned as Maya, dressed in a bright orange minidress, appeared, camera in hand. 'Wow,' she said, looking at the results on her phone screen. 'That kid, sorry, my god-daughter, is a natural. Your mum takes a good photo too, Dante. This one of her pinching one of the waiters' bottoms is classic.'

'Oh, God, Maya, delete that right now,' Beatrice gasped.

Her sister twisted away as Beatrice went to grab her phone.

'We said no phones.'

'I'm exempt, and, anyway, Carl made me do it and he's royal.'

'You're impossible.'

Dante came up behind her and slid his arms around her waist, pulling her into him until he could rest his chin on the top of her glossy head. '*This* is my family and all that I need. A tabloid would pay good money for that snap, Maya.'

'Now he tells me.'

Grinning, Dante bent and whispered something in his wife's ear.

He laughed, loving that she could blush... loving her.

'You know, I used to think this place was a prison, but you opened the doors, let in the light that made me love you and set me free.'

'Oh, get a room!' Carl exclaimed, walking in.

It was a palace—they had a lot to choose from!

* * * * *

If you were head over heels for
Waking Up in His Royal Bed
*you'll love these other stories
by Kim Lawrence!*

A Cinderella for the Desert King
A Wedding at the Italian's Demand
A Passionate Night with the Greek
The Spaniard's Surprise Love-Child
Claiming His Unknown Son

Available now!